THE HOLLYWOOD HIGH CHRONICLES

book 1

Intuition

by **Melissa Velasco**

ISBN 978-1-7365373-5-0   (paperback)
ISBN 978-1-7365373-6-7   (eBook)

1st Edition

Models contracted through DMe Talent Agency:
Deidre Michelle (Agent) @dmetalentagency11

Models: Maddie Dawn Cordero, Julian Gopal, Versai Knight, Isaiah Romero Cordova, DeAngelo Bethea, Justin Graham, Angelo Almanzar

Makeup and Hair: Xavier Visage
Costume Consultant: Trey Pickett
DeAngelo Bethea Costume Design: Trey Pickett
Costume Design: Melissa Velasco
Cover Concept: Melissa Velasco
Photography: Tino Duvick @brokenchainphotography
Cover Design: Tino Duvick and Anna Hall
Interior Design: Anna Hall
Editing: Kyle Fager and Mary Beth Kite

Dedicated to my friends from Hollywood High School.
We remain forged in a brotherhood and sisterhood that
only that unique place could create.

INTUITION

CHAPTER 1

A throng of students moves up the walkway to the front doors of the main building. Hollywood High School looks like a Golden Age of Cinema palace, perfect in its classic 1920s-glam-covered-in-a-little-grunge kind of way, a statue of languishing beauty in a world that zooms too fast. Even from the curb, I can sense its secrets and mystery.

I flow with the crowd, folding myself into the crush of motley salmon swimming upstream. Suddenly, I'm an actual student filing toward a building that has housed the crème de la crème of Tinseltown. In red and black block lettering, the giant banner hanging over the door reads WELCOME TO YOUR 1992–1993 SCHOOL YEAR.

A glimmer of hope flares to life in the back of my mind. *If I could become me anywhere, it's here.*

The front entrance hallway is wide and smells like floor wax. Table after table lines the hall, each one representing a different station in the strange orientation dance of the first day of school. I slide into the long line at the table with *Magnet Schedules* written artfully on a poster board taped to the wall. Energy swirls from the jostling students all around me.

Panic rises, and my palms sweat.

The wall to my right is decorated with big red stars bearing names of the who's who of showbiz who attended *this* school—so many recognizable names that the cluster of stars stretches out of sight around the corner. They speak to me, whispering of promise, telling me I belong. I close my eyes and try to slow my racing heart.

Keep your cool, Mel.

The line moves quickly, and I step up for my turn.

An ample woman with jovial energy is ready with a greeting. "Good morning. I'm Ms. Gilley, your school counselor, but everyone calls me Ms. G. What's your name?"

"I'm new," I blurt out. *Way to cut to the chase, Mel.* "I apologize," I add awkwardly. "I'm really nervous. Melanie Slate. It's nice to meet you."

Ms. G smiles and hands a piece of paper across the table.

My schedule.

"Well, Melanie," she says, her tone vibrant and encouraging, "your grades are impressive, and your theater and dance experience is certainly in keeping with our expectations here at Hollywood High School for the Performing Arts. When we reviewed your application, we felt you were an excellent candidate. Competition is fierce, and we're incredibly selective. Work hard to keep your spot."

Fear, self-doubt, and loathing suddenly enter a death match in the back of my mind. The effort to ignore these ever-present hinderances threatens to make me sweat through my shirt. I've already been worried I'm not good enough to be here, so Ms. G's challenge is almost enough to tip me over the run-and-hide edge. I take a shaking breath, a gargantuan effort given my social anxiety, and blurt, "The first time I saw this school five years ago, I got chills from head to toe. I know it sounds weird, but sometimes I intuitively know things . . . before they happen. This is where I'm literally destined to be. I promise to make you proud."

Though the bit about my supercharged intuition is absolutely true, I'm positive I just sounded like a moron. *Socially awkward, as usual.* A blush creeps up my neck, and my face burns fuchsia. I smile, trying to rally.

Ms. G grins and snorts. I scurry out of the way and duck my head as the redhead behind me smirks.

Sigh.

Down the hall, beside the big red star hand painted with the name "John Ritter" in fancy gold lettering, there's a vacant spot. *Someday, maybe they'll put my name up there.* I roll my eyes at myself and scoot out of the crowd to check my schedule.

FIRST PERIOD	*Algebra – Mr. Martinez*
SECOND PERIOD	*Biology – Ms. Becksworth*
THIRD PERIOD	*History – Ms. Marley*
FOURTH PERIOD	*English – Mr. Bentley*
FIFTH PERIOD	*Int. Jazz – Mr. Isley*
SIXTH PERIOD	*Theater – Ms. Ferry*

This is going to be a long day, grinding through four core courses before I get to my dance and theater classes. The time on my pager says seven-forty, twenty minutes until the first bell. Plenty of time to explore. Through the double doors into Quad Two, I skirt the edge of the crowd and head for Actors' Alley, the place where my summer tour guide told me the Magnet students hang out. Campus looks so different than it did during my summer tour. I can't believe how many students are here. These are *high school* kids? They look like adults . . . or space aliens from another planet. Piercings, rainbow hair, studded leather jackets. One of them zooms past me on a Harley, so close I have to leap back. Without even a sideways glance at me, the rider veers toward the side parking lot.

How am I going to fit into this world? I'm screwed!

At once, all my self-assured "this is my destiny, be the new me" nonsense dissolves, and that old familiar crippling terror creeps up from my gut.

Think, Mel. I glance around like prey in search of a place to hide. *There!*

Just before the fight-or-flight response sends me reeling through the churning river of students, I hear a voice.

"Hey! Girlie! Come here!"

No way that voice is calling to me. I turn slowly and discover that it's coming from an older boy lounging on a picnic table along the edge of Actors' Alley. He sports a head of wavy brown hair, and is wearing black slacks, a white button-down dress shirt, and a thin black tie. I catch myself gaping openly at his perfection.

He crooks a finger my way, his mischievous eyes flashing. "Come on! I don't bite . . . much." He laughs, tinged sinister.

The hair on the back of my neck stands on end, my intuition sparking to life. *Your intuition is never wrong. Don't trust this guy.* But then again, I'm supposed to be the new Mel. *This guy's giving me a lifeline.* Uncertainty wars at the back of my mind. I ignore it as I wander closer to him. He pats the spot beside him on the table, and I gingerly sit.

"So, gorgeous, you're new, huh?"

I nod shyly.

"You have a name, right?"

I gulp. "Melanie. Today's my first day." I close my eyes and will the old Melanie to crawl into her cave at the back of my mind.

Mystery Boy says, "I'm Joel Stamp." Then he adds, with an arrogant air, "I'm the student council president, and you're one lucky girl to have met me."

Is this guy serious? My stepfather always says that I hide nothing, every emotion playing across my face. My skeptical gaze slides Joel's way. *He's arrogant, but the student council president must be popular.* A split-second decision tells me to ignore the nagging intuition and give this a shot. "Lucky me," I say, smiling a bit too brightly. "How long have you been a student here?"

He leans back, posing like a male model in a prom ad. "I'm a senior." He pauses to regard me contemplatively. "I've decided that you get to go on a date with me after school."

My heart skips a beat. I've never been asked on a date before. Then again, he really didn't ask me. He definitely *told* me to go on a date with him.

That doesn't seem right, but . . .

My thoughts are interrupted by an irritated voice.

"Well, looky what we have here. Joel's at it again." The boy approaching us looks like a worldly hippie meerkat straight from an avant-garde production of *Alice in Wonderland*. Next to him strides a taller guy wearing an edgy black trench coat and sunglasses with round lenses, his raven hair artfully pulled back in a curly ponytail. Both newcomers project the air of the aggressively miffed. Sexy Meerkat glances my way, pity flashing in his eyes in the instant before he turns back to Joel with laser focus.

"Up," Meercat growls. "This is our table."

Both guys move in closer and toss their backpacks on the table like they're claiming territory.

I hop up, giving them space. *Nice one, Mel. You've been here all of twenty minutes and already have two people glaring at you.*

Joel makes a show of putting his arm around me. The gesture snaps me out of my self-pity as my skin crawls the tiniest bit. He turns and steers me away. Sexy Meercat and his friend send us off with a death glare.

Silently, Joel leads us past group after group of students excitedly greeting each other after a long summer away from school. My intuition's screaming at me to run, but it's swept away on a wave of insecurity. My head starts to swim, regret boiling in my stomach. *I'm in over my head. What made me think this school was a good idea?*

Joel waves to a large group of kids ahead, and immediately I notice that the guys are wearing the same outfit as him. *Must be a student council uniform.* They're accompanied by a group of sexy schoolgirl drones, all in black pleated short skirts, black stiletto heels, and white button-downs. The girls smack me with a collectively snotty expression. In my head, I sigh and brace. I know their type all too well. Still, I try to rally, taking a deep breath and smiling.

"What's up, my man!" Joel slaps hands with his closest fashion clone, a tall, thin boy with a military buzz cut and a face full of freckles. The boy would be adorable if not for his perma-sneer.

Buzz Cut aggressively turns his focus my way. "Who's this?" His tone evokes an odd combination of amorous interest and haughty disgust that makes me instantly wary.

"This is Melanie," Joel says. "She's new." He introduces me to Buzz Cut, whose name turns out to be Stan.

The guys all regard me with bored disinterest, but the girls close in around me with a saunter. Their big, pretty eyes brim with malevolent curiosity.

The leader, a curvy, raven-haired beauty, appears the least willing to give me the benefit of the doubt. "Are you a Regular or a Magnet?" I must look confused because she rolls her icy eyes and explains, "Regulars are students that live around here. The *real* students who belong at this school. Magnets are the performing arts losers who have to beg to get in. So, duh-face, are you a Regular or an intruder?"

Duh-face?

Her friends all snicker and circle around me, menacing arrogance radiating from every preppily clad girl. It's like being trapped in the middle of a teenage secret service circle, and every fiber of my intuition is screaming at me to run.

"Um . . . well, I'm a Magnet. But I'm new and don't know anyone, if that helps." I try to make myself look as unthreatening as possible, which isn't hard because I feel about an inch tall. If I'd been a ghost in my junior high life, now I've become something worse. A speck.

"I'm Victoria," says the snot in charge. She bats her eyes at Joel. "You can play with her all you want, but she's out. No Magnet's infiltrating our group. Besides, her outfit's pathetic."

"Can it, Victoria," Joel snaps back. "You're repeating the ninth grade. I'm not interested in the opinion of an idiot."

The bell rings, and my fly-under-the-radar years of training take over. I scurry away while the Drones are still grabbing their backpacks. I slide into the swift-moving tide of kids heading toward the two-story building. My schedule's in my back pocket, but I'm not about to check it for fear I'll trip or run into someone while my attention is drawn. The crowd's jockeying, people skirting off right and jostling left. Everyone but me seems to know where they're going. My heart starts racing again, and my throat's tightening with looming tears. I'll die of shame if I cry in the middle of this crowd. I need to find a quiet corner somewhere in this mayhem and get myself together.

I'm practically trampled trying to get through the double doors of the two-story building. A tough girl in a leather jacket gives me a dirty look for accidently bumping into her. My apology gets interrupted by an elbow to the head from a tall kid carrying a boombox blasting "Breed" by Nirvana. I manage to duck and dodge into a little alcove under the staircase across the hall.

Tears spill down my cheeks as I lean on the wall under the stairs. *Why did I apply to this school? I have to get out of here and call my mom.* I'd spotted a bank of pay phones on the back side of the commons building as I was jostling through the crowd. *I'll wait here until the bell rings, and then I'll make a run for them.*

Suddenly, Joel appears by the stairs. He's moving commandingly through the crowd in my direction. A short boy runs headfirst into him, and Joel grabs the kid by the front of the T-shirt, his handsome face contorting into a vicious sneer. He freezes mid-motion, his fist pulled back to hit the kid. He glances my way and eases off as the awareness that I'm watching creeps in. He releases the boy and gallantly apologizes to him before pushing his way to me. I'm caught in an alarming limbo between suspicion at the flash of aggression and relief at no longer being alone.

"You disappeared, beautiful." Joel reaches out, wiping tears from my cheek, then puts out his other hand. "Let me see your schedule. I'll walk you to your first class."

Shyly, I reach into my back pocket and get out the schedule. While he looks it over, I pull myself together, wiping my face, running my fingers through my hair and straightening my backpack on my shoulder.

"I can't attest to the loser performing arts classes," Joel says with a smirk, "but I know that your first-period algebra teacher's a jerk about students arriving late. We better book it upstairs."

He puts his arm around my shoulder, and we head through the

thinning crowd. My breath catches a little as I glance slyly up at him. He really is handsome in a Clark Kent kind of way, with a hint of a dimple on his right cheek as he shines a devastating grin back at me.

At the end of a long upstairs hallway, he stops in front of a classroom and turns to face me. He sweeps the hair out of my eyes and runs his hands down my arms, the featherlight touch giving me goosebumps. "Your second period's downstairs, just past the staircase around the corner. You can't miss it."

The tension floods from me now that I know where I'm headed.

"I'll meet you at the end of your second period and walk you to third, okay?" he says.

I give a shy nod. *Maybe my intuition is wrong for once. He's not so bad. He's helpful and definitely cute.* "Thank you. I was starting to think I can't do this."

Joel tips back his head and laughs. "You can do this. Give it a week, and me and you will be king and queen of this place."

My heart races. I've never even been noticed by a guy, and now this senior's interested in me? He leans in, cupping my chin, and I melt. Just as he starts to move his lips toward mine, a girl's voice rasps at us, startling me into taking a step back.

"Found another victim already, huh, Joel?"

In unison, Joel and I turn toward the uninvited distraction. I experience a strange mixture of disappointment and relief. The look on the girl's face adds a third layer to the conflicting emotions: suspicion. *What does she know that I don't?*

I size her up quickly. Heart-shaped face, body so voluptuous that my eyes nearly bug out of my head, confidence that I've never even dreamed of having. I can't compete with this girl. As I'm spiraling down a shame vortex, her green eyes are boring seething hatred holes into Joel. If looks could kill, he'd be obliterated.

Joel exudes indifference, cold and ruthless. "If it isn't Presley Verelle," he says. "I see your bitchy demeanor hasn't improved over the summer."

Presley disregards the slight, turning to face me like a snake targeting a new victim. I steel myself for a witty verbal assault. Unexpectedly, her expression softens from malice to concern. She sighs and slowly shakes her head before stomping into the classroom.

Joel's eyes are black with rage as he watches Presley storm off. Then, his expression performs that same unsettlingly rapid shift I first witnessed when he decided not to pummel the boy downstairs.

How does he morph between such conflicting emotions so fluidly?

He smiles at me, winks, and heads down the hall, leaving me at the classroom door just as the tardy bell rings.

CHAPTER 2

First period couldn't end soon enough. The teacher's a misery, and I'm baffled how someone can fly through instruction so fast while being such a grump. My second-period biology class is exactly where Joel said it would be, which raises my spirits—right up until the moment I step inside the room and notice that several of the Drones are clustered at the back. Victoria, the prettiest of them, notices me and rolls her eyes. I fight the urge to return the gesture, recognizing how it would be a smart long-term decision to fly under Victoria's radar.

I spot an empty desk as far away from the Drones as possible, but before I can claim it, a wiry kid with greasy hair slides into the seat. He gives a blank look when he notices me standing next to him, his red stoner eyes hooded from the weight of too much smoke.

All right, a new plan.

I survey the room, finding that most of the seats have been eaten up by students who moved faster than me. The only spot left is in front of Victoria. The thought of that viper sitting behind me for an hour makes me nervous, but short of sitting on the floor, there's no other option. I hesitantly make my way through the crowded row of desks to the regrettable spot in front of my new best enemy. I set down my backpack and slide into the seat, careful not to make eye contact with her.

An unsubtle whisper drifts my way on a wave of her pricey perfume, followed by a torrent of giggles from her two friends.

Wonderful. Let the gossipy girl games begin. I sigh and rub my forehead. At least I'm in familiar territory. Being the target of jerks isn't new for me, and I've become an expert at ignoring their taunts.

Thankfully, the teacher—a mousy-looking librarian type with thick glasses—stands behind her desk and claps her hands twice, calling us to attention. She introduces herself as Mrs. Becksworth as she divides up a pile of worksheets and then hands a short stack to the first student in each row.

The shuffling sound of papers accompanies a flurry of worksheet passing, and as the stack reaches me, I feel my hair move slightly. I snap my head around to catch Victoria holding a wad of gum between her fingers. *Ah yes, the old gum-in-the-hair trick.* "Really, Victoria?" I say with an acidic tone. "Gum in the hair?" I dump the stack of worksheets on her desk and whip around, leaning forward and pulling my chestnut brown hair over my shoulder, hopefully out of her reach.

The trio of Drones giggles and gasps.

This is going to be a long school year.

The worksheet is a list of "get to know you" questions. Some are simple—phone number, address, parents' names—but at the bottom is a more advanced layer of prying curiosities.

"What do you hope to accomplish in high school?" is the first essay question, and I wonder if "survival" would be a suitable answer.

I focus on the page in an effort to ignore the energetic cattiness behind me. For a first day assignment, this worksheet is an easy one. I finish just before we all hand our papers up to the front of the room.

After the bell rings, Joel, to my relief, is waiting for me outside the classroom. He's watching Victoria, who beat me out of the room and is now leaning in a sexy pose, like a cheap sleaze, against a bank of lockers down the hall. We watch as a guy walks up to her, and she squeezes her arms together to accentuate her voluptuous chest.

I'm not usually one to stare because it attracts the kind of attention no self-respecting social ghost would ever want to draw, but something about this boy intrigues me. He's around five foot nine, black hair, tan complexion. He's beautiful. I wonder what the hell a guy like him would want with scum like Victoria. I don't have to wonder for long because she pushes away from the lockers and slinks and swirls toward him, oozing sexual prowess. Yup, there's no doubt what he sees in her.

Sigh. There's at least one of these girls at every school, and they're always trouble.

"Victoria has your attention, I see," Joel says.

I can't help but roll my eyes. Joel chuckles as we watch the handsome boy attempt to ignore Victoria, who is essentially throwing herself at him.

Victoria, having apparently heard Joel laughing, stalks toward us. Her lady Drones and the hot guy follow. The girls are shooting ice daggers my way.

Freaking awesome.

The hot guy stops next to her and glances from Victoria to me with a suspicious expression.

"Been meaning to ask you this all day," Victoria says to me, her arms folded over her chest. "*What* are you wearing? You're so pathetic!"

I glance down at my white shirt, jeans, and white Converse. I roll my eyes, and the insecurity I'm accustomed to slides away. I'm left glaring at Victoria. Her hot guy tilts his head to the side, seeming curious about my shift.

"You're such a joy, Victoria," I quip. "Being a shallow monster becomes you."

She looks shocked and glances from side to side at her Drones. "You should just leave now and go back to whatever school you came from."

My eyebrows rise and I snort. *Is she serious?* I close my hand, checking my palms for their usual anxiety sweat, but they're dry. *Interesting. Looks like I really am starting to change for the better.*

Victoria moves toward me, attempting to aggressively back me up against the lockers, but I refuse to move. We end up nose to nose. Confusion flashes across her face just as the hot guy puts his hand on her shoulder and pulls her back.

She glares at me. "New plan," she calls to her Drones. She turns to me and smiles in challenge. "One way or another, you'll leave."

She snaps her hand over her head in what I assume is some teenage "Queen Bee" domination ploy, and I can't help but laugh.

"You've clearly seen *Heathers* too many times," I tell her.

Liltingly, she says, "We're out, girls."

They saunter down the hall in their black skirts and white blouses, their stiletto heels clacking with every step.

The hot guy doesn't follow Victoria. Instead, he looks at me, his eyes narrowed in amusement. There's something intriguing about him. We lock eyes for a moment, and an electric charge pulses between us. My intuition sparks heavy with anticipation, and I gasp. His eyes widen. There's something about this guy. He winks at me subtly before turning and walking down the hall.

Interesting.

Seemingly oblivious to the moment I just shared with Hot Guy, Joel grins. "Well, you just earned an enemy for life. Victoria's pissed."

I snort. Then curiosity gets the best of me. "Who's the guy she was talking to?"

Joel shrugs. "No one. Just a local kid. Flavor of the week."

He's trying a little too hard to appear indifferent. *Looks like they aren't exactly friends.*

Joel puts his arm around me and steers me down the wide, crowded hallway before rounding the corner toward my third-period classroom. We stop in front of the door.

"I've escorted you to your next class, my lady," he says with a gallant air.

"Any hints on this one? So far, you've been dead-on."

He throws back his head and laughs. "Your mission, if you choose to accept it, is to stay awake. Monotone Marley's the name, and soul sucking's her game." He squeezes my hand and heads to a classroom down the hall, turning to appraise me one last time as he passes through the doorway.

CHAPTER 3

Joel was right again. Monotone Marley makes my first-period teacher seem like a riveting delight. The bell finally rings for the conclusion of the longest hour of my life. I rub my eyes, fighting to fully recover. Time to head out and see if Joel's waiting for me.

Outside the classroom I find a sea of rushing students, but no Joel. *That's okay. I think I know where I'm headed.* The bungalows are just beyond the exit doors ahead. It's easier this time as I make my way through the crowd. It occurs to me that this is no different than walking just about anywhere in Los Angeles. I grin at the silliness of my panic this morning. I wind and weave, ducking and scampering around the passing crush.

The heat of Southern California midmorning hits me as I exit the two-story building. I head down the stairs and look left, scanning the bungalows for classroom numbers. *All odd. Nope, I'm looking for bungalow four.* I spot the right classroom, and as I approach, Presley, standing in the doorway, raises an eyebrow.

"Hey, Joel-bait," she says. "You in Mr. Bentley's class?"

I nod, only slightly perturbed by the unwelcome nickname.

"It's this one," she says.

Wonderful. Once inside, I see instantly that the kids in here are different. All are creatively dressed, and they're laughing and talking enthusiastically. The energy is just right.

I belong here.

"Why don't you sit with me and Marcus?" Presley suggests.

I size up the potential of Marcus, who's looking at me with pleasant curiosity. He seems okay, his expression almost jovial, so I quickly decide to take Presley up on the invite.

As soon as we're all seated, Presley and Marcus lean toward me.

"I've been dying to talk to you about Joel," Presley says. "You got brain damage or something?" Her tone holds no menace. Instead, she seems amused.

I can't help but laugh. "You likely know more about him than I do. Fill me in."

She side-eyes Marcus, who smirks.

"He's an ass," she says. "I'm talking world-class jackass."

My eyebrows rise. Presley's assessment is pretty close to my original instincts about Joel. "Elaborate."

"He's threatening on a good day and dangerous on a bad one."

I clear my throat, my mouth suddenly gone dry. "I had clues he was off."

Marcus speaks up like a game show announcer. "Ding, ding, ding. We have a winner. Presley, tell her what she's won." He gestures with a flourish to Presley.

"You've won a potential one-way trip to Rape Town," Presley says. "Next stop is Gossipville, where your reputation will take a nosedive."

My eyes grow wide. "Aren't you a freshman? How do you know all of this?"

There's no mirth in Presley's grin. "I've known some of the students here a long time."

Before I can ask anything more, Mr. Bentley starts his lecture.

Fourth period goes by in a flurry. Mr. Bentley is hilarious, and I regret having been so consumed by the heads-up about Joel. I would've enjoyed more of Mr. B's anecdotes if I hadn't been so distracted.

When the bell rings, Presley and Marcus rush off.

I gather my stuff and exit the classroom. Today's been heavy. I need some alone time. There's a place I've overheard a few of the kids talking about in the hall—a private, shady spot they call Smokers' Corner. Seems like it has promise for a slip-away lunch.

I ask the nearest kid where I can find the place. He eyes me skeptically for a moment before giving directions. I set a fast clip and don't slow my pace until I'm well past Quad Two. My palms are sweating, and my stomach's knotted with the kind of anxiety that always lives just below the surface. Halfway there, I'm winded, but it's worth it for some peace and quiet. *Dang, this is a long walk! No wonder the smokers don't get caught; no out-of-shape teacher is going to hoof it all the way over here.*

The crowd is relatively small, each person eating on their own, reading a book, and listening to music through headphones. Surveying the area confirms I've chosen the right place to find some peace and quiet. I could use a smoke, and I have a book in my backpack that's been neglected for far too long.

As I draw closer, only a few of the smokers even bother to glance up, their expressions impassive. Apparently, strangers aren't discouraged. I scan the grove in search of a spot, and my gaze settles on a guy on the edge of the grove leaning against a tree with his back to me, his knee up, balancing what looks like a sketch pad on his leg. His sandy-blond hair wafts gently in the breeze. His leather jacket is well worn, likely not chosen as a cool statement piece, but, rather, as his oldest friend. That's when I recognize him from my arrival that morning. He was the guy on the Harley that nearly plowed me over.

I realize almost too late that I've wandered closer than I intended. Could be the smell of his Cool Water cologne, or that his hair glints a hundred different shades in the sun. I'm close enough to tell that he looks and smells like California sunshine and an ocean breeze. My head swims, and I can't think.

What the hell's wrong with you? It's just a boy.

But no. It's more than that. A wave of interest rolls through me.

If I'm already this close to him, then I have to know what he's sketching. I decide to walk by, subtly glance at his sketch pad, and then head to the bench across the way. Shade would be nice, and I can keep a sly eye on him from there while I eat.

One glimpse of his drawing—a moonscape beach with the ocean in the distance—stops me dead in my tracks. How he has created such depth and detail with just a pencil is beyond me, but the picture is captivatingly real, alive on the page.

Okay, Mel. Gazing over his shoulder all lunch period isn't part of the plan. Keep walking.

Making my way to the bench is a process. I'm in a daze, my heart pounding in my ears like the crashing of his sketched waves. I nearly trip on a tree root. I make it—barely—take a seat, and relearn how to think. The act of reaching for a cigarette from the front pocket of my backpack proves an excellent distraction. I make a mental note that I need to run past the bowling alley down the street from my house and buy a fresh pack from the vending machine that no one ever prevents minors from using.

One step at a time, Mel. Cigarette to mouth, search for lighter.

"You need a light?" asks a voice that's too close for comfort.

I startle, and the cigarette drops from my lips. I hadn't heard anyone approach, but my head's been in the clouds—clouds that smell like Cool Water cologne. "Damn." I look down to find the cigarette, and my gaze falls on a pair of motorcycle boots, capped by a pair of ripped jeans.

I scan higher to a plaid flannel, artfully knotted at the waist. The boy is sporting a perfect six-pack under his tight white tank. At this point, I'm committed to the ogling. Hell, I've already taken in every inch of him from the waist down, so there's no sense in playing it cool. I notice with a growing mix of fascination and horror the perfectly broken-in leather jacket draped over the white tank. Long neck, strong jaw, and then I'm gazing into a pair of ocean-blue eyes.

Oh. My. God. He's gorgeous. Gorgeous! Can't breathe, can't think, can't make words. I get lost in his eyes, feeling like I'm falling.

He stares back at me, unblinking. He rattles his head, as if to clear it.

I see his lips moving, and I realize with a start that he's asking me a question. *Get it together, Mel!* "I'm sorry, what?" I ask.

He bends to pick up my cigarette, looks up at me from his kneeling position, and smiles. "I said, 'Do you need a light?' And then I asked, 'Are you new here?'"

He's amused. Is that good or bad? He must think I'm a freaking idiot!

Suddenly, I recognize that I have a choice to make. I can either sit here like a mute statue or I can try for sheer honesty. "I'm sorry," I say with a coy smile, "but you seem to have rendered me speechless."

A hint of a smile plays at the edges of his mouth. He seems intrigued. "Really? Why's that?"

Okay, I can work with this. Time to catch his attention. I zip up the little pouch on my backpack and stand, forcing him to stand with me. I sling the backpack over my shoulder and snatch my cigarette out of his hand. "I'd love a light," I say, putting it to my lips.

He snaps open his Zippo, and the smell of butane mixes with his cologne—sexy and dangerous, like bad choices and driving fast down dark roads. I decide in an instant that he smells like my type. He strikes the flint and I lean in, gazing at him through the flame. I hold his eyes for a touch longer than I should.

"Thanks." I wink and turn on my heel to walk away.

"Hey, wait!" he says, his voice a little gravelly. "You didn't answer my question."

I continue walking, while turning back to look at him. "Why was I rendered speechless? Because you're gorgeous!"

I face forward again with a parting wave, and strut off with my hips swerving. When I feel his eyes on my body, it's like an electric current stretching thin between us.

As the distance between us grows, I hear a low, sexy chuckle behind me.

I'm feeling pretty satisfied with myself as I round the corner of the bungalows and run into Presley. She's with a beautiful blond girl wearing a tight burgundy tank dress and Doc Marten boots. They're chatting with the guys who confronted Joel before school. Trench Coat chuckles as I get within earshot.

"Hey, isn't this Joel's new girl you were talking about?" he asks Presley.

Their blond friend hits the guys with the ultimate disappointed-mom look, her pretty blue eyes flashing.

"She isn't Joel's girl," Presley says. "She just happened to meet him first."

Sexy Meerkat squints in my direction. "You must have the worst luck in the world. But if you play your cards right, your luck might take a sharp turn. I'm Hiram Friedman, and this is Arch Terani." He points to Trench Coat.

"Ar*ch*?" I ask.

"It's pronounced 'Ark.'" He gives Hiram a good-natured shove. "Like Noah's Ark. My actual name's Angel, but you'll see soon enough how unfitting that is. When I was little, I got the nickname Archangel, and it eventually got shortened to Arch."

Hiram steps forward and drapes his arm over my shoulder, setting a brisk course through Quad Two with Arch, Presley, and the blond girl following close at our heels. "You don't think we'd let you eat alone, do you? Oh nooo. I've decided that you're our entertainment today, and we plan to find out everything there is to know about you."

Oh no! No, no, NO, NO, NOOOOOOO! Being the center of attention might be worse than eating alone!

Unsure how to respond, I go with, "Who's *we*?"

A few minutes later, I find myself seated in the middle of a rather fascinating group of vibrant personalities at the table where I met Joel before school. This is apparently *their* table, and I'm hoping it might become my table. I'm surprised how nice Arch and Hiram seem, given our initial introduction when I was with Joel this morning. A girl named Valerie Merser is sitting next to Arch. She's a gorgeous senior with wavy long blond hair and shockingly strong confidence to support her tough-girl demeanor. Next to Valerie sits Kenji Gwan, an effortlessly easygoing type who doesn't talk much—but then again, that may be because the blond girl, whose name turns out to be Finley Farell, is filling all the airtime, animatedly telling a fast-paced story, her hands waving about, keeping the rest of us in stitches. Next to me is Presley, and on her other side is Marcus, whose last name is Vinsky.

When Finley finishes her story, Hiram shushes the group. "All right, Melanie. You're up. We want to know everything there's ever been to know about you, right now." He leans forward, grinning as everyone nods.

I sigh, rub my forehead, and look down at the table. My face gets hot as a dreaded blush betrays how little I enjoy being in the social spotlight.

"Aw, she's shy," Arch says. "Come on, out with it."

Everyone laughs.

I snort softly at the expressions on their expectant faces. "You guys are giving me a lot more credit than I deserve. Getting accepted to Hollywood High is literally the most interesting thing that's ever happened to me."

All eyes, practically unblinking, are on me.

"Okay, here it is in a nutshell. I was born in Texas. My parents got divorced when I was little. When my mom married my stepfather, Rich, we moved to Los Angeles. I've been basically friendless ever since. I spent all three years of junior high as a ghost. I've been in every play and dance class that I could find over the past nine years. I like theater because I get to become someone else. It's a break from being Melanie . . ." I trail off, having said more than I intended, and sheepishly look down at my lap. "I'm sorry to go on and on. Like I said, I'm not that interesting." Suddenly, I want to ooze into a puddle under the table.

Kenji, Hiram, Marcus, and Arch are all leaning on the table with their hands under their chins, grinning at me like cartoon birds sitting on a wire.

"I'm interested," Hiram says flirtatiously, and the other guys all chime in, "Me too," in unison.

Valerie guffaws. "Cool it, guys. The girl's sitting here wanting to die because she had to talk about herself for thirty seconds, and you goofs are turning this into an episode of *The Dating Game*." She turns to me. "Ignore them." She rests her chin in her hand. "For a self-proclaimed ghost, you've now managed to attract the attention of five guys at the school in less than a day. Not that Joel counts." Her lips pull back into a sneer as she glances behind me. "Speak of the devil, and he might show up!"

I look back and see Joel approaching. My heart sinks.

Valerie slides out from between the bench and table and stands. Everyone but me joins her. "Don't worry. We've got your back. Leave Joel to us."

Joel stops ten feet away, his hands on his hips as he takes an aggressive, wide-legged stance. He extends his arm and points a finger my way. "She's *mine*!" he growls at the group, radiating unexpected menace.

My mouth drops open. *Uh-oh*. A version of Melanie that I usually keep a tight clamp on boils and roils from my depths. There's nothing I can do to stop her before she acts. I rise up and whip around, marching to Joel. I don't stop until I'm nearly nose to nose with him. "What did you just say?" My eyes narrow and my lips pull back in a furious sneer.

Taken off guard, he stumbles back a few paces. My new friends gasp and laugh behind me.

"Damn!" Valerie says. "I like her. I can work with this."

"Yeah," Presley says, "I had a feeling about this one."

In any other circumstance, I would have reveled in their praise, but now, I only have eyes for Joel. "I don't know who the hell you think you are, but I'm not yours. I don't even know you, and frankly, I don't like the little bit I do know. You're an arrogant blowhard, and your friends are ass—"

Arch puts his arm around my shoulder, cutting me off before I can finish the word on the edge of my lips. "You need to pick on someone your own size," he says to Joel. "Because I do believe that Melanie's out of your league."

Joel stares at me, fuming. He opens his mouth several times, looking like a fish out of water, but no words come out. Finally, he turns and storms off, chased away by the sound of my new friends' laughter.

I'm worried about what the others will think of my outburst as I slowly turn back to them, but they're all grinning. The adrenaline drains out of me, and I smile back. A nearly hysterical guffaw escapes my mouth. Suddenly, I'm more alive than I've ever been. I haven't felt this good in years. My prison of insecurity and exhaustion has been blown wide open, and I'm no longer suffocating.

"Well *hello*, Melanie!" Valerie says. "You fit right in with our crew. Everyone is scared of Joel, except us."

I give a remorseful smirk and look down at my outfit. "I *wish* I fit in. You're all fierce and fabulous, and I'm just . . ."

A look passes between them like a secret from one to the next—a silent game of Mental Telepathy Telephone. That look somehow becomes an unspoken plan. A borderline scheme crackles through the air, and out pours an unexpected invite to go on what Arch refers to as a "Hollywood Boulevard quest to get what you need." Judging from their enthusiasm, the group lives for these excursions, and my mousy newness is reason enough for another. I'm tempted, but then my heart sinks. There's zero way my parents are going to allow their fifteen-year-old to wander Hollywood Boulevard with strangers.

But . . . this is exactly what I need. *It's worth a shot.*

After some thought and a quick walk to the pay phones, I drop a quarter in and dial the number for home. The group stands around me, anxiously hoping I'm allowed to go. They listen to my side of the call as Mom answers.

"Hi, Mom. It's Melanie."

"Oh no, is everything okay?"

"Everything's really good, actually. It's a long story, but I've met a group of friends and—"

"A group?"

"Yes. There's Finley, Presley, Kenji, Hiram, Arch, Valerie, and Marcus."

"*Seven* friends?"

"Yes, seven friends."

"That's so exciting!"

"Yes, Mom. I know it's exciting. Listen, they've invited me to go shopping with them on Hollywood Boulevard after school . . . for clothes."

"But you have clothes."

"Yes, I know I have clothes, but I don't exactly fit in around here. We're thinking you could pick me up around eight at Snow White's Café on the Boulevard. We want to have dinner together after we shop."

"I don't know, Melanie . . ."

"Mom, if you saw these guys, you wouldn't be worried. Nothing's going to happen to me with them."

There's a long silence before she finally—shockingly—agrees to let me go.

"*Really*? Oh my gosh, Mom! You're the best."

"Do you have any money for shopping?"

"Yeah, I've got my savings money from my allowance on me. I promise to get something good."

She goes into a long rant about how proud she is of me, and I just hope my new friends can't hear it through the receiver. Then she says that she and Rich will pick up the dinner check for the whole group when they come get me.

The offer is so good that I rush off the call before she can change her mind. "Thanks, okay, bye!" I hang up and squeal. "We're a go." I explain the situation about Snow White's and my parents offering to cover the check. "I can't believe she agreed to this."

Everyone's grinning as Presley says, "You *really* must have been friendless for your mom to agree to let you wander around in the ghetto with strangers *and* pay for dinner."

I smile sheepishly.

"Okay," Arch says. "Everyone hightail it to the lunch table after sixth period. We'll meet there."

CHAPTER 4

How has every class flown by almost maniacally, and now sixth period has lasted three and a half years? I can't focus on anything except the prospect of wandering Hollywood Boulevard with my fascinating new friends.

The bell in . . . three . . . two . . . one . . . *I'm out!*

There's no dallying in gathering my stuff this time. I'm gone, first person out the door. I bolt down the four-story flight of stairs along the outside of the theater auditorium building, practically skipping to the table to wait for my new friends. Quick at my heels are Marcus and Presley, bantering back and forth about some story from this summer.

Everyone arrives in record time, and the group sweeps me away toward the exit gate. We head down Highland Avenue toward Hollywood Boulevard. Together we stretch the width of the wide sidewalk, each with his or her own unique style and flair. Walking through the streets of Hollywood is just another Monday afternoon for them, but I'm hard pressed to play it cool. *Seriously. I'm doing this? A sheltered Texas girl wandering the streets of Hollywood with a group of people so uniquely cool they should be in a movie?*

The effort to fit in takes every ounce of my attention. *Don't screw this up! Head high. Laugh when it's funny. Don't stand out!*

We turn left onto Hollywood Boulevard, where I'm hit by the grungy, seedy reality of this place. Homeless people, street musicians, tourists, and odds and ends from all walks of life crush and press into us. The group falls in behind Arch, who is a force of nature in his black trench coat with an anarchy symbol hand painted in red on the back. His confident stride easily cuts through the crowd. He's the only one walking alone, and he seems perfectly fine with it, an alpha wolf with cool glasses and a pierced ear.

Being with these people is strangely easy. Any shop with promise is fair game, and this merry band of misfits is better at finding the right clothes than any movie stylist—especially Hiram and Arch, who have a wicked eye for affordable pieces. In a particularly intimidating shop full of everything rock 'n' roll, Valerie, Finley, Hiram, and Arch carefully select items that for the life of me I can't see going together. Valerie grabs my arm and drags me into a dressing room, smiling mischievously as she closes the stained curtain behind us. The cramped space is so disgusting that I have to work hard not to shudder and run.

If I want to fit in, I have to do this. Strip down in front of a girl who intimidates me. Try on this bizarre pile of clothes. Sigh. Here goes.

The clothes somehow feel like they fit, but there's no mirror in this raggedy dressing room. I dread having to strut out in front of everyone in this getup. What if I look like a clown? Or worse, what if I look like a little girl playing dress-up? *Oh God, I'm going to die of shame. All these kids look like adults with their curvy hips and movie-star hair, and I'm going to come off ridiculous in this.*

Valerie, on hands and knees, laces up the heavy Doc Martens they've selected for me. Then she gazes up and grins a slow, almost vicious, smile, one eyebrow rising like an exclamation point.

"Hell *yes!*" she yells. "Hey, losers, we did it." She puts a hand on my hip, spins me around, and shoves me out through the curtain with a gentle whack on the tush.

She laughs bawdily behind me.

I don't have time to ponder what this means because I stumble through the curtain into the waiting arms of my new friends.

"Well, hello, hot stuff!" Hiram catcalls. "Get a load of you!"

I pause to wonder if he's being sarcastic, but then I notice Arch's slack jaw, Kenji's smile, and Marcus's raised eyebrows. Finley's bouncy squeal punctuates the point.

Presley is the only one with no expression. She stalks toward me, hips sashaying. She spins me around and puts an arm over my shoulder. In the mirror, I catch a glimpse of her admiring gaze as she looks me over.

"Welcome to the world, Mel," she says. "You're one of us now."

I stare at my image in the mirror, and it's like I'm seeing myself—my true self—for the first time. *Unbelievable! How did near strangers manifest my inner soul in such perfect outer covering?*

CHAPTER 5

The bus arrived early on Friday of the second week at my new school, so I have time to enjoy my walk and take in the energy of Hollywood High. I consider waiting at my group's table, but I want to be alone. My social battery's at empty. The last two weeks have passed in a flash, and my new friends have kept me busy. I'm not used to so much socializing. I'm always running and dodging, never getting to really experience this place. There's a strange magic in Hollywood, a town full of hopes and dreams, chaos and failure, and Hollywood High's no exception.

Unhurried, I make my way across the quad to the two-story building. The daily rush is starting as the halls fill with people. At the top of the stairs, I come face-to-face with a pack of Joel's thugs.

That jackass Stan has Daniel by the front of the shirt. Daniel squeals as Stan slams him into the lockers. My heart stops. My palms break out in a panicked sweat triggered by my years on the receiving end of vicious school bullies.

"Give it to me *now*!" Stan yells, pulling Daniel back and slamming him into the locker again at full force.

The hall is full of kids doing nothing more than watching the show. Every face looks scared. *What is* happening *around here?* The stranglehold that the student council bullies have on the school is insane. *Can't any of these people see we outnumber the Drones and could end this?*

I gather myself, clamping down my terror. "Enough!"

"I-i-i-i-i-i-i-m-m-m-m-m o-o-o-o-o-o-k-k-k-k-k-a-a-a-a-y, M-m-m-mel-a-a-a—" Daniel's in my second-period class. He's one of the most brilliant kids at the school, but he has a stutter he battles daily. The more nervous he is, the worse it gets, and under this much duress, it's the worst I've ever heard it.

Stan cuts him off with a mimicked "I-i-i-i-i-i-i-i-" before slamming his back against the lockers.

I march over to stop the conflict, but Joel brushes by me and moves in beside Stan.

"Give it to me, Stutter Boy, or you're going to regret it!"

Joel screams so loud it makes me stop and close my eyes. An avalanche of panic overtakes me. *I have to do something.*

When I open my eyes, I spot Arch and Marcus running up the stairs. Arch wedges in between Daniel and the two bullies. Joel lets go of Daniel and rounds on Arch.

Arch is ready for him, dodging Joel's flying fist before giving him the slightest shove that sends him stumbling down the hall. "What the hell do you think you're doing to my buddy Daniel?" Arch yells.

Marcus slides between Daniel and the pack of Drones, who've been watching the show, and holds them there with a glare.

I rush to Daniel, who is slumped in a heap on the floor. "Daniel, look at me."

He stares at the floor, and I can see tears welling before he blinks them away. He puts out a hand and meekly pushes me away.

His face is a bright shade of pink made more prominent by his flaming-orange curly hair. He doesn't say anything, but it's obvious he wants to disappear into the floor. I sigh, closing my eyes. I know exactly how he feels because I was him in junior high. It's unbearable living life as a target, knowing there could be an enemy around every corner at a school you detest.

I turn back to the confrontation down the hall. Even though only seconds have passed, things have shifted for the worse. Arch has Joel pinned to the floor, but Marcus is in trouble. Stan and three other Drones have him surrounded, all leaning forward. The energy in the hall is electric. Marcus is tough, his face cool and calm, but he's outnumbered. Everyone in the hall knows what's coming.

I rush over, intending to help, just as Tanner Devick appears at the top of the staircase. Tanner's an odd cat. He's known for his wild outfits and makeup, and he has an androgenous sexiness about him. I stop short and point in Marcus's direction. Tanner rushes into the middle of the circle and stands next to Marcus. *Interesting.* I wouldn't have suspected Tanner of being so noble, but having bounced into the fray, he's now flashing a vicious grin.

"Hey, Marcus," Tanner says casually. "What's happening, my man?"

Marcus grins at him and they square up, back-to-back, taking on two Drones each. Stan lunges and chaos ensues. He lands a right hook that rings Marcus's bell. Tanner bum-rushes another Drone, but the Drone's friend counters, shoving Tanner off-balance.

I hear Valerie's voice before I see her round the corner at the far end of the hallway. Her speech falters as she realizes what's happening. She, Hiram, Kenji, and Finley all pick up the pace and rush in to help. Suddenly, it appears our odds have improved.

Time to take a stand. Together we wade into the skirmish, and the Drones are quickly put to the floor.

"Aw, come on, guys!" Hiram says. "Don't give up so easy. Hop up and let's go another round."

We all laugh. Leave it to Hiram to be hilarious in the middle of a school brawl.

Knowing they're outnumbered, the Drones back up and slink down the hall.

"This isn't over," Joel says over his shoulder as he walks off.

Hiram claps his hands. "Yippee! More playtime!"

I laugh, shaking my head, before turning back to Daniel. He has managed to get to his feet and must have gathered his scattered textbooks during the face-off. As he leans against the lockers and clutches his books to his chest, he looks exhausted, his sunken eyes staring blankly at the opposite wall.

Arch goes to him and the rest of us follow. "What did they want from you?" he asks.

Daniel answers slowly, his words deliberate and without his usual stutter. "They've been stealing my money for lunch and the city bus. They find me every day and take it. I wouldn't give it to them today. I'm sick of not eating and having to walk an hour and a half to get home after school."

Arch claps him on the back. "We'll keep an eye out for you, man. Any time you think there's trouble coming, just come and find one of us. We'll help you out."

Daniel nods and mutters, "Thanks," before plodding down the stairs, his head hanging, dejected.

Arch turns to us with a frown. "This is ridiculous. I'm sick of the Drones, and I'm going to make a plan."

Val raises an eyebrow. "I love when you get pissed. What are you thinking?"

"I don't know yet, but those guys are dangerous and need to be dealt with."

As I pass through the door to his room, I nod to Mr. Martinez, but he doesn't respond. He has the personality of an algebra equation. Nothing but nonsensical letters and numbers, empty of compassion, governed by rules not understood by those of us with a heartbeat.

I take my seat and watch as my classmates trickle in. Some are bleary-eyed and holding coffee. Others look like supermodels. A few clearly rolled out of bed and slogged their way here wearing yesterday's clothes.

Presley stomps in looking harried and generally bothered. Both of us hate math, and starting the day with algebra puts a damper on her mood. She takes her seat and huffs before dragging her math book out of her backpack. Then she closes her eyes, tips back her head, and murmurs, "Anywhere but here."

I can't help but laugh because she goes through this every morning. We've got a whole school year of this, and it would make more sense for her to give in to the inevitable with good humor, but that isn't in her nature. Presley's our Dylan Thomas girl, all kinds of *Do not go gentle into that good night. Rage, rage against the dying of the light.*

The bell rings, and Mr. Martinez closes the classroom door. Anyone left in the hall is screwed due to his strict NO TARDY policy. *He must be a miserable man. Who else gets his jollies torturing fifteen-year-olds all day inside an un-air-conditioned building?*

As Mr. Martinez picks up a stack of worksheets, the loud-speaker crackles to life.

"Good morning, Hollywood High! This is your theater director, Ms. Ferry. Homecoming is only a few weeks away. Be on the lookout for posters advertising our homecoming dance. And, with no further ado, it's time for . . . homecoming court nominations!" She spouts this last bit with the theatrical flair only someone of her career choice could muster. "Your first-period teachers have the nomination forms. You may only nominate students from your own grade. Think carefully! One vote each! All votes will be tabulated, and the top three boys and top three girls from each grade will be put on a ballot to be handed out today during third period. Teachers, please have a student deliver your completed nomination forms to the theater office as soon as possible. Thank you!"

Dang! This school moves quickly.

Clearly put out, Mr. Martinez begrudgingly hands the nomination forms to the first person in each row. The forms are handed back from person to person, and then the usual shenanigans start.

Marcus announces, loudly, from across the room that he plans to nominate, "Your mom, and your mom's farts."

"Charming," Presley says under her breath with a roll of her eyes.

She must be in a particularly bad mood this morning. Usually, she's right in the middle of Marcus's nonsense, laughing and joking along with him.

The red form has two spots, one for a princess and one for a prince. The prince's name is easy. Marcus will win. There's no question about that. I write in his name, and for good measure, I write in Presley on the princess line. She glances at my paper and then looks at me with a softer expression, clearly cheered up.

Good. Today will be easier if her mood improves.

We pass our completed forms to the front.

"Volunteer?" Mr. Martinez barks, waving the stack of red papers over his head. "Theater office."

"Me, me, me, me!" comes a squeal from the back of the room.

I don't have to turn around to know it's Mandie. Every class has the "Ooo, ooo, ooo, pick me!" person, and Mandie is ours. She flounces to the front of the room in a purple bubble skirt, pink jelly shoes, and a top that reads *Reach for the Stars*.

"Can I kill it?" Presley hisses, the words intended for my ears only.

I laugh too loudly.

"Is there something funny, Miss Slate?" Mr. Martinez asks. Joy is his kryptonite, and laughter isn't allowed in math class.

Instead of answering, I opt to look down at my math book and rearrange the papers on my desk. Under my breath, I say, "Definitely."

Presley snorts.

My third-period chair has a loose bolt. Every day, the damn chair pinches the skin on my leg, and every day, I try to shift into a new position that avoids the welting torture.

Monotone Marley not so enthusiastically claps her hands to call the class to attention. She's simultaneously interrupted by the screech of feedback over the loudspeaker and a knock on the closed classroom door.

"Hello, Hollywood High! Your nominations have been tabulated. The top three homecoming royalty candidates from each grade are now ready for your votes. Choose carefully! Your votes will determine your 1992 homecoming court. Winners will be announced on Monday." Ms. Ferry's chipper voice disappears.

I turn my attention to the front of the class, where Ms. Marley starts handing out a stack of papers, still warm from the copier.

All right, let's get this over with.

For homecoming prince, the choices are Marcus Vinsky, Tanner Devick, and Shane Smith. I'm going with Marcus.

For princess, the choices are Presley Verelle, Victoria Garcia, and—

Wait! What?

There, on the red paper in front of me, clear as day, is the name Melanie Slate.

Me? I'm nominated?

I circle Presley's name and glance up from the page to find the whole class looking at me. My anxiety flares, and my palms break out in a slimy layer of sweat. I wonder if the students in Victoria's and Presley's classes are staring at them.

I look away, trying not to acknowledge the scrutiny, and spot Joel glaring at me through the window in the classroom door. He's laser focused, radiating evil from his piercing eyes. My breath catches and my chest constricts as my intuition blazes to life. I fight the impulse to double over around the pain in my chest, positive my classmates will wonder what's wrong with me. Joel's unblinking stare sends fear racing up my spine.

This guy's really off. Dangerous. And he knows where my classes are . . .

Ms. Marley starts her lecture, and Joel slides out of view. I sink in my chair, my thoughts scattering, as I try to assess how much potential trouble I'm in with this guy.

CHAPTER *6*

Heaven help me, Ms. Marley can sure drone on. How can that woman make something as fascinating as the Civil War so painfully dull? History has always been my favorite subject . . . until now. I must have drifted off, my brain fighting to survive the never-ending waves of soul-crushing monotony, when I hear my name. Given Ms. Marley's tone, I clearly missed a question and then several "Melanies" before the one that dragged me from my cyclonic fretting about Joel.

Without thinking, I reply sarcastically, "Again, with gusto!"

The class snickers.

Monotone Marley gawks at me like a cartoon cow that just got kicked.

Before her near-retirement brain can catch up, I quickly add, "I apologize. I was so captivated by your lesson that I missed the question. Please ask again."

She stares at me with sharp ferocity. Not as dumb as she looks, apparently, which is a shame because it means she's actually *choosing* to bore us to death with her dull teaching methods. It makes me think less of her. I've been taught that it doesn't matter what you do in life; your objective is to be the best you can at whatever that is. Dig ditches for a living? Fine! Shovel hard and fast. Ms. Marley's a crappy ditch digger, and young minds are paying the price for her lack of passion.

I slit my eyes a little, knowing that I'm playing with fire, and wait for her question.

"What year was the Emancipation Proclamation signed? The document that freed the slaves? As I'm sure you paid attention to my lecture."

She spits out the last line with a layer of sarcasm, her beady eyes hard and penetrating. She thinks she has me pinned. She's wrong. I didn't spend years as a mousy introvert, lost in a land of books, and learn nothing.

"January 1st, 1863," I reply. Then I hit her with it: "But the Emancipation Proclamation wasn't that simple. Your lecture doesn't do that genius document justice. The Emancipation Proclamation was a trump card played by Abraham Lincoln in hopes of ending a Confederate political standoff. Confederate states seceded from the Union, and Lincoln promised them compensation for freeing their slaves, but only if they rejoined the Union. If they didn't rejoin, then the slaves would be freed with no compensation given to the landholders. Confederate states didn't rejoin, and so Lincoln signed the order only freeing slaves in Confederate states. He didn't free slaves in the Union right away. I believe it was William Seward, secretary of state, who said, 'We show our sympathy with slavery by emancipating slaves where we cannot reach them and holding them in bondage where we can set them free.'"

She's already staring at me slack-jawed when I hit her with the final uppercut of knowledge.

"So, Ms. Marley, Abraham Lincoln used the Emancipation Proclamation as a bargaining chip, and when it failed, he had a secret poison dagger written in. Manipulative American politics at its finest. I'm sure you knew all of that, though, given that this is your profession and all."

I snap my mouth closed with an audible pop and meet her eyes with ferocity. This woman prides herself on mediocrity, so I don't regret my tone. Just when the silence becomes deafening, the class erupts with hoots of laughter.

Marcus, perched on top of his desk, says, "Can *she* teach the class? That's the first time I've understood anything in weeks!"

Ms. Marley looks prepared to detonate. Her red face scrunches up, she inhales, and I know I'm in for it. Just as she opens her mouth to let me have it, the bell rings.

The clang seems to deflate her. She sags in her chair and visibly gives up.

Did I break her? Damn. I just wanted to test her a bit, not kill what was left of her spirit. *Sigh. I need to work up an apology.*

CHAPTER 7

I spot Victoria whispering something to a kid holding a skateboard as she passes him in the hall between periods. Victoria throws a smirk my way before exiting the building and disappearing in a halo of sunlight.

She's up to something.

I turn on my heel, but before I can take a step, I'm promptly stopped by the grungy scrub—greasy hair, red stoner eyes, dirty Guns N' Roses T-shirt, skateboard tucked under his arm.

I frown. *What does this kid want?*

"You're Melanie, right?" he says.

"Yes. What?" I don't have time for this.

"Wanna go to the homecoming dance with me? We can get a hotel room after . . . 'cause I wanna get to know all of you." He motions with his hands as though tracing my curves.

It's too difficult to process the nastiness of that thought, so the only thing I can do at first is blink repeatedly. I might have a sharp mouth on me lately, might have become a bit bold, and might smoke the occasional cigarette, but I'm *still* a lady.

I pull myself together. "You need a shower, enrollment in an etiquette class, and a whole lotta prayers before *any* of that's going to happen."

Skater Guy sneers, and I turn to leave.

"Bitch!" he calls after me.

His brand of stupid is about the last thing I want to engage with right now. If he becomes a problem, I'll send Arch his way. We'll see how he likes dealing with someone who's wicked social vicious and knows how to turn the school against problem people.

The building exit isn't far. Sunshine streams through the doorway, cheerfully illuminating the dingy hallway. I cross the threshold and draw in a cleansing breath.

"Hey, gorgeous!" comes a voice from behind me.

What in fresh hell? I've got to get to class!

I look back, and my eyes meet Joel's. This is the cherry on top. Joel creeped me out less than an hour ago, and now he's standing here acting like everything is normal. It's freaky and unsettling.

"Hi, Joel." My tone makes it clear I'm exhausted with his bullshit. "What's up?"

"We got off on the wrong foot. I'm here to ask you to the dance."

He says this with a haughty air that sets off alarm bells in the million-year-old lizard part of my brain, triggering my fight or flight instinct and filling my bloodstream with adrenaline.

Tread carefully, Mel. "That's really flattering," I say. "I wish you'd gotten to me sooner. I've already accepted an invite to the dance. But thanks for thinking of me."

His faces falls. He seems to have bought my story. I politely scoot past him, mentioning that I'm going to be late. Joel says with creepy conviction, "I'll be seeing you."

The hair on my arms stands on end, and I hightail it down the four steps and through the rushing crowd. My heart doesn't stop pounding until I round the corner of Quad Two and am clear of Joel's gaze boring a hole in my back.

What a creeper!

This whole homecoming court nomination thing is crazy. During the last leg of my journey to class, four more dance-date hopefuls, all strangers, stop me.

All received a polite, "No, thank you."

I'm staring off into space, lost in worry about Joel, the plethora of dance invites, and how rude I'd been to Ms. Marley.

Marcus brings me back to reality. "Earth to Melanie! Come in, Melanie."

"I don't think that's what they're saying," Presley says. "Think about it. *Thrice to thine and thrice to mine and thrice again to make up nine. Peace, the charm's wound up.*"

I rub my bleary eyes. We're in English class, tasked with translating Shakespeare's Macbeth into modern language. Mr. Bentley has divided the script among us, and we have to read our versions together on Monday.

Marcus scratches his head, confusion playing on his handsome face. "I don't get it. I'm trying, but this is just a bunch of noise to me." He reaches into his backpack for a Twizzler. He always seems to have more snacks than school supplies in his bag. He's like a walking vending machine. I guess when you have the face of Adonis, you don't have to try at school.

Presley, one side of her headphones off her ear, taps her pencil in rhythm to a Nine Inch Nails song, the music playing just loud enough that only our group of three can hear it. "Bottom line," she says. "The witches are devious. Best characters Shakespeare ever wrote. Dusty-ass story has some meat to it."

I set my head in my hand, puzzled, as I look over the passage again. This scene's as tough as the others have been. The characters have so many layers. Add to that the complicated Shakespearean language, and it's a trip.

"Essentially, the witches are saying, 'Three from you, three from me, three from she! The spell is set. Don't worry. It's happening.' But we have to make our version sound good." Presley absently extends her left hand and waves in Marcus's direction. "Give me a Twizzler. I'm going to figure this out."

It seems gnawing on the end of the candy vine brings inspiration because she tosses off her headphones and starts writing. Everything Presley writes is genius.

Marcus smiles at me from across the table, while his head bobs to NIN's "Terrible Lie," streaming from Presley's discarded headphones.

Presley has just started writing her rendition of the scene when the door opens and the classroom is flooded with sunlight. Half the fluorescent lights above are turned off, and along one wall of the room, there are windows with the shades pulled closed. That's the way Mr. Bentley likes it. He says it keeps the performing arts vampires to a dull roar. He cracks me up.

I'm temporarily blinded by the light, but when the spots clear, I see Tanner standing at the front of the room, staring at me. Tanner spends most of his time in a smoke cloud, writing poetry and wandering around. Today's the first time this week he's graced the class with his presence. I rarely talk to him, so it's beyond me why he's suddenly, so intently, fixated on me.

"Tanner!" Mr. Bentley booms with a hint of amusement.

"Welcome to class! To what do we owe this rare pleasure?"

"What's hanging, Mr. B? Thought I'd drop in with some news." Tanner shoots a devious glance in my direction before continuing.

Something's up.

He saunters about the room, running his hand across the closest desk and snagging a pencil from Susan, who huffs. Susan's always worked up about something.

Tanner dramatically stops at the back of the class and turns with a flourish. The whole class swivels in their seats to watch the performance.

He gestures in my direction and aims his finger seductively my way. Everyone turns to glance at me and then back to him.

"Melanie has done a hero's duty!" he announces.

What is he talking about? I don't have time to be amused by my classmates whipping their heads back and forth between Tanner and me. I'm consumed trying to figure out what I've done.

"Thanks to Melanie's third-period takedown, Monotone Marley just quit!" He sprints to me, dropping to his knee and bowing his head like a courtly prince. "How can we ever repay this act of kindness? The entire school owes you a debt of gratitude."

He leaps to his feet and continues his speech. Mr. Bentley likely should have shut down this insanity long ago, but there he sits, smiling and chomping on one of Marcus's Twizzlers.

"*No more* boring lectures! *No more* nodding off in class! *No more* calls home because I don't care about her blah-blah-blah. The torture's over, people! Monotone Marley is *history*." He slaps his leg, belting his stoner laugh at the pun.

Oh no! I sit in my seat, but I'm a million miles away. I don't particularly enjoy Ms. Marley's class, but I don't hate the woman, and I definitely hadn't intended to push her over the edge. I took things too far, and now I won't even get the chance to apologize.

Just when I've sunk quite thoroughly into a guilt spiral, I realize Tanner is standing in front of my desk again.

For the love of God, what now?

"Mel, seeing as how I owe you for getting rid of my biggest problem at this school, I would like to ask . . . drum roll, please . . . would you go to the homecoming dance with me?"

Confidence brims in his red-tinged eyes.

What the hell? Is he seriously asking me in front of the entire class?

I look across the table and see twin expressions of glee on Marcus and Presley's faces. *Evil!* They're supposed to be my friends, yet there they sit, relishing every second of my nightmare.

I clear my throat and think fast. "Tanner, that's a really sweet offer. How about we talk about it tomorrow at lunch after I can ask my parents tonight?"

This seems to satisfy him because he pumps his fist, gives me a quirky thumbs-up, and then flops bonelessly into his empty chair.

"If we have no further announcements," Mr. Bentley says, "please get back to desecrating the fine work of Shakespeare!"

The class returns to the dull murmur that always accompanies group work. The attention is off me, finally. I pull up my hoodie and thump my head on my desk.

"Barely got out of that one, girl," Presley says.

I peer up into her amused green eyes. She lives for the cringe-worthy experiences of others and is loving this.

"What's the deal with this dance?" I ask.

Presley breaks into a half smile. "Yeah . . . our student council sucks. The homecoming dance is in two weeks, and they haven't even advertised it yet. We've got the court nominations in full swing, but nothing at all about the details of the dance."

"Well, Mel, *I'm* not asking you," Marcus says playfully. "I have my eye on a different girl. One so sugar-sweet she could melt in the rain." He leans toward Presley and bats his eyes. He looks like Pepé Le Pew trying to woo Penelope.

I can't help but snicker at the look on Presley's face.

"I already said I'd go with you, so give it a rest," she says. Then she smiles in what I assume is her brass-knuckles version of flirtation. "You sweet talker, you."

"You two really are cute," I say with a grin.

Presley chuckles. "Mel, you have bigger things to worry about than how cute we are. You have to figure out how to let down *Dazed and Confused* over there. I mean, the guy's charming in a hot David Bowie kinda way, but he's not your type."

"I know. Ugh. Maybe he'll forget by tomorrow?"

"Not like-ly," Marcus says, punctuating each syllable with a wave of his Twizzler. "He's gazing at you like you're the last bong on Earth. And let me tell you, Mel. He wants a hit."

CHAPTER 8

My friends surround our picnic table. I'm late to lunch because of another series of homecoming date proposals. I must have been stopped twenty times trying to get here. The situation has moved past flattering, through bewildering, and now it's just plain annoying.

I hear Arch, Hiram, Marcus, and Kenji plotting their escape from school as I approach. The new Alice in Chains album hit store shelves today, and they're ready to execute the ditch plan they've been scheming up for a week.

"Val, will you cover for me in fifth and sixth period?" Arch asks.

Val smirks. "Sure. I'll tell Mr. Chase you have cramps and had to go home."

We all laugh, but Arch, forever shameless, doesn't take the bait. "Give it a shot. It's worked for you a thousand times."

The boys head to the gate by the back stairs of the theater building. The security guards haven't caught on that someone—a certain trench-coat-wearing deviant—stuck gum in the door latch. It no longer locks but appears to the unsuspecting eye to be secure.

This is my chance to get some information. Since the first day of school, I've been dying to get the girls alone to grill them on what they know about the Harley guy. He's been living rent-free in my head for weeks.

"So," I say, "there's this boy—"

Finley's enthusiastic squeal cuts me off. She does this anytime gossip is about to be revealed. "Do tell!" she says with twinkling eyes.

Presley, lounging on the table bench, snaps her fingers and sarcastically sings, "Tell me more, tell me more, like does he have a car?" A real modern-day Rizzo, that one. She rolls her eyes, radiating, *Bored now.*

"Actually, he has a Harley," I say.

Val and Presley clamber to their feet. Finley stiffens. It's not exactly the reaction I expected.

"His name's Adam Stone, and he isn't a boy," Val says, emphasizing the point with a jab of her finger. "He's a monster. Mel, *no.*"

"You don't want to go there." Finley's approach is gentler than Val's but laced with as much conviction. "He's nothing but trouble."

"He can't be that bad," I say, uncertainty creeping into my tone. "He smells good . . ."

Finley and Val start jabbering at once, each determined to steer me clear of Adam. I can't understand most of what they're saying, each talking over the other, but their message is clear: they do not approve.

Presley cuts through the din of teen angst. "He *is* that bad. He's the school's resident player. Don't let that pretty face fool you. He talks a good game, but he has no actual interest in you. Conquest is an addiction with that one. Once he knows he has you locked, he'll get bored and chase after the next bunny that bounces across his path."

They all nod in unison.

"Exactly what she said," Val offers. "He's bad news."

"How many people do you actually know that he's done that to?" I ask skeptically.

"Ladies?" Val says as if asking for a survey from the group.

Three hands go up.

"He's done it to all of us," Val continues. "He always calls his current conquest 'Missy' because he says it's easier than remembering their actual names. I was Missy two years ago, Finley was Missy last year, and Presley did a brief stint as Missy in July."

"We went to the beach," Finley says, a little starry-eyed. "It was worth it."

Val elbows her, and Finley snaps out of it, saying, "I mean, he's awful. You shouldn't pursue this."

As if on cue, I hear a Harley in the distance. The sound gets louder, bouncing off the buildings, as Adam turns the corner into Actors' Alley. He stops by the fire-escape stairs, cuts the engine, swings his leg expertly over the back, and lounges against the bike. He's looking straight at me. We're too far away to speak, but his eyes speak volumes.

Victoria chooses this moment to slink into Actors' Alley. She stops a few feet away, and the four of us shoot her a dirty look. She runs her hands suggestively down her sides and bats her eyes in Adam's direction—an over-the-top flirtation. Finley and I exchange a pitying glance as we watch Victoria's pathetic preening. Victoria cocks a hip and wiggles for Adam's benefit like a sexy cartoon squirrel. He watches her and his eyebrows rise, clearly amused. His mouth twitches, and I have to give him credit for not openly laughing at her. My group can't say the same for ourselves.

"The only thing missing from that mating dance is a swishing tail," Valerie quips.

Amused, we all smirk.

When Adam looks back my way, Victoria follows his gaze. Her seething glare settles on me. Before I can react, she storms my way, heels clacking, hips swirling dramatically. She stops in front of me, challenging with a wide-legged stance.

She points over her shoulder in Adam's direction and snarls, "You don't have what it takes to interest a stud like that." She giggles, gives a fake purr, and then fires a come-hither look back at Adam.

The sexy boy leaning against his Harley tips his head to the side, eyebrows furrowed, clearly baffled.

I can't help but laugh. "Looks like Adam isn't picking up what you're putting down," I say to Victoria, giving her an amused grin.

She narrows her gorgeous eyes at me. "You need to leave. There's only room for one queen bee at this school."

"Hornet, Victoria," Valerie says. "You're a horny hornet, not a bee."

Victoria huffs and stomps her stiletto. "I hate you," she snarls at me.

"Hey, Victoria!" comes Adam's voice.

A surge of anticipation causes her to quiver. Victoria turns toward him and cocks her hip.

Adam grins. "Can you move? You're blocking my view."

Victoria's eyes nearly bug out of her head. She wheels around and hits me with a death glare. I return her glare with a blankly innocent look and a shrug. Then I slide a smoldering gaze Adam's way.

After Victoria storms off, my friends start hissing at me in low whispers. I vaguely gather that they want me to grab my backpack and follow them into the music building, but I can't wrap my mind around it. The smell of Harley fumes and warm sunshine fills my head, and everything disappears except Adam's blue eyes.

He crooks his finger nonchalantly at his hip, gesturing for me to come to him. That's all it takes. All common sense goes by the wayside, all uncertainty vanishes. I grab my backpack and walk toward him.

"Mel, *no!*" comes Finley's worried hiss behind me, but it isn't enough to stop the tide pulling me to Adam.

The closer I get, the bigger he smiles. It's a dangerous smile— the motorcycle is dangerous, and the boy is clearly dangerous. He swings a leg over the bike, fires up the engine with a roar, and reaches out a hand to me. He doesn't say a word. I have zero clue where he's headed. I've never ditched school before, and now I'm leaving on the back of a stranger's Harley. None of that seems to matter because I watch my hand move to his, watch my leg swing over the seat, watch him pull me onto the back of his bike. His muscles strain against the leather jacket, and he places my hand on his shoulder before letting go.

"Helmets?" I ask.

Adam cracks up.

Well, all right. I guess when you're young and hot, you don't wear helmets, even though it's illegal.

With a slight turn of his head, he says, "Hang on, Missy. It's gonna be a wild ride." He guns the engine, circling my friends, all of them statues of worry and disgust.

He flips them the bird as we take off.

We make a right into the alley, a right onto Highland, and then he guns it. Sunset Boulevard roars up on us. Adam takes another right at breakneck speed. He finally slows from Mach 20 to Mach 10, and I relax a little. The Sunset Strip, with all its billboards, tattoo parlors, and shops, sprawls before us, and I am riding down this iconic street on the back of a gorgeous guy's Harley. A thrilling bolt of excitement shoots up my back, and I decide there's no sense in being scared. You only live once, right? But the better part of me whispers in the back of my head, *I hope we live to see tomorrow.*

We pass Tower Records just as Hiram, Arch, Marcus, and Kenji, bags in hand, emerge through the glass doors. I guess the Alice in Chains CD wasn't sold out yet. *Good. Maybe it'll distract them from the story about seeing me on this motorcycle.*

They look up at the sound of the Harley as Adam guns it to get through a yellow light. I see Arch point to us, and peer back over my shoulder as their worried faces turn to watch us pass. They do not look happy, apparently sharing the girls' opinion that this guy is a monster.

Looking back is disorienting. I turn to face front, putting my forehead against Adam's leather coat. I've dealt with car sickness for as long as I can remember, and now I can add motorcycle sickness to the list. My stomach's suddenly at war with my equilibrium.

If I throw up down the back of Mr. Monster, I'll die of shame.

I focus on my breathing, and my stomach starts to settle just as Adam steers the Harley into a right-hand turn. I glance up at the street sign. Laurel Canyon. *Oh boy.* I've gotten sick in my stepfather's minivan more than once on this winding road.

Adam guns it, and suddenly, all fear of losing my lunch evaporates, chased away by the fear of losing my life. We're racing the canyon, taking turns at lightning speed, and I quickly figure out how to lean with Adam into the turns.

He glances at me over his shoulder and flashes a genuine smile.

He looks younger, his face bright with joy. I scoot closer to him, my arms around his waist, so I can feel his muscles bunch in the direction of each curve. We zoom down the road going God only knows where, and for the first time in my life, I feel like I'm flying.

CHAPTER 9

The Harley rumbles to a stop at the light at Ventura Boulevard, where we make a left and crawl with the traffic for a time before Adam pulls into a spot on the street and parks. We've apparently reached our mystery destination. I swing my leg stiffly over the bike, stumbling a bit, unpracticed at the motion, and move out of the way so Adam can get off.

He smiles and makes it look easy.

His arm over my shoulder, we head down the sidewalk to a coffee shop with a sign that reads *Insomnia*. I've never heard of this place. Adam pulls open the intricately carved wooden door, and as soon as we're inside, I find myself overwhelmed by the perfection of this place. Dark wood-paneled walls lined with bookshelves. Overstuffed armchairs in elegant jewel-toned velvet. Candles lit in sconces. The intoxicating smell of espresso. It's like the place was transported from the 1800s.

The weight of Adam's arm leaves an electric pulse that lingers after he removes it to reach for his wallet.

"What'll it be, Missy?"

I try not to chafe at the nickname as I study the menu. I settle on an iced vanilla latte and a blueberry muffin. Adam orders, and we head to a velvet, ruby-colored love seat. As we settle in, it suddenly occurs to me that I don't have a clue what to talk about with this guy. What little I know about him isn't good—player, user, schemer.

My mom's voice is in my head. *Beauty is only skin deep.*

He's beautiful, but is there anything under that perfect skin that *is* deep? I study him as he takes off his jacket and tosses it unceremoniously onto the arm of the love seat. As the barista delivers his coffee to the end table, he turns to me, his face set in a sexy smolder that I suspect is his go-to expression reserved for the Missies.

"So, Missy . . . new girl, huh?" He's careful to meet my eyes.

Cute. The old "look her in the eyes and pretend to be interested" act. Let's see what I can do to throw Mr. Monster off-balance. "You do realize that my name isn't Missy, right?" I raise an eyebrow and a slight smile plays on my lips. In an effort to avoid eye contact, I stare down at the latte and muffin the barista left me on the table in front of us.

"Um . . . okay . . . then what's your name? Or should I just call you beautiful?" Successfully, he has managed to rally into another tactic. Charm.

Huh-uh, Mr. Monster. I'm not getting played that easily.

"Does that actually work? The whole 'charming suave guy who's impersonal and mysterious' act?" Now that I've made it clear I'm not buying his crap, I'm starting to question my choices. I watched this guy take down Victoria viciously—granted, I can't exactly hold that against him—was warned about him by people I trust, watched him flip off my friends, and left with him having no clue where I was headed.

He looks slightly perturbed, but he shifts into a relaxed pose, arm over the back of the love seat. His expression transforms into an innocent pout.

Another tool in his arsenal. Is this guy ever genuine?

"Aren't you the inquisitive one?" he says. "Yes, the cool-guy act usually works, but I can see that you're a rare girl. Which *me* would you prefer?"

The ether has worn off. I'm starting to get uncomfortable. Call it buyer's remorse. I want to go back to school, but it seems the only way to make that happen would be to bite the bullet and let my mom know where I am. She won't be thrilled.

"I'm going to run to the restroom." I stand and subtly check my pocket to make sure I have change. Satisfied that I have a quarter or two, I shuffle toward the bathrooms, hoping there's a pay phone.

I'm in luck. There's one tucked in the corner at the end of the hall. I pick up the receiver, drop in the change, and dial.

"Hello?" Mom's voice drifts over the line in an optimistic tone. Hopefully, my stupidity won't ruin her good mood.

"Mom, please just listen," I blurt out as quickly as I can. "You can blow up later, but I'm in over my head right now, and I need help."

When I hear Mom inhale, I close my eyes and prepare for the explosion.

"Rich, get the car keys!" She's holding the phone away from her mouth so she can yell into the house. "Melanie's in trouble!"

Rich is home? I didn't anticipate that. My heart races. He's not likely to be amused about my ditching school.

"All right, kiddo," Mom says. "What's wrong?"

Relief floods my body and I exhale hard. "I ditched school with a guy who's turned out to be a questionable choice. I'm on Ventura and Woodman at Insomnia Café. I'm safe here. We're having coffee, but I don't want to leave with him. He doesn't know I'm calling you. He thinks I'm in the bathroom."

"She's at a place called Insomnia Café on Ventura and Woodman with some charming punk," I hear her relay to Rich. "We have to go get her right now."

"Give me the phone." Rich's voice rings out deadly serious over the line. "Melanie, what's going on?"

I take a deep breath, ready for his upcoming lecture, and explain the situation.

"How is it not going well?" Rich asks. "Be specific."

Suddenly, I'm unsure, and it occurs to me that I don't really have a solid answer for Rich's particular question. "I guess I'm just uncomfortable."

Rich's tone lightens. "Has the guy actually done anything dangerous while you've been with him?"

I think for a second. "Well, he drives a Harley."

A short laugh barks over the line. "Riding a Harley in a city with the kind of traffic we have makes this guy smart, not dangerous. I rode a Harley for twenty years, Mel." He pauses before adding, "You know what I think? It sounds to me like the old Melanie's crawled back to the surface because you feel guilty about ditching and got scared. There's nothing wrong with that. Change takes time. But, Melanie, new experiences are part of growing up."

"Are you kidding?" I hear my mom say. "If she says she isn't safe, then she isn't safe. We're going to get her!"

"Carol, I'm telling you there's a difference between being in danger and being uncomfortable in a new situation. She's never ditched before, and she's out with an older guy. It's okay for her to be uncomfortable, but let's not get this twisted. There's a young man's reputation on the line." Rich moves the phone closer to his mouth and addresses me again. "All right, Melanie. I know Insomnia Café. Expect us in thirty minutes."

"I'll be here, but there's no way you'll arrive in thirty minutes."

Rich must have handed the phone to Mom, because she's the next to speak.

"We'll be there in thirty minutes, Melanie," she says, her voice tight with concern. "Rich just said he knows a back way."

"How much trouble am I in?" I'm close to tears. This is one of those moments that I realize I'm not as grown-up as I thought. I've been fooled by a taste of high school freedom. One of my first independent decisions, and I folded the second I got nervous. My parents might not ever trust me again.

"You aren't in trouble. You're going to make mistakes, and I'm proud of you for calling us for help. Although I do see Rich's point. You ditched school, which I'm not thrilled about, but we'll discuss that later. Stay where you are, and we'll be along shortly." Mom pauses, but I can sense she's not done. "Go back and sit down with this boy before he gets suspicious. Pretend you're surprised when we get there. We'll play it cool because there's no point in your reputation getting destroyed by him knowing you called your parents to rescue you."

As she says goodbye and hangs up, I'm left there in shock. Their response was the last thing I expected. I stand there holding the receiver, realizing they're right. There's a big difference between being in danger and being uncomfortable. I vow to do a better job of handling my own issues from now on. Valerie and Presley wouldn't have called their moms to rescue them just because they found themselves in uncharted territory. They would have taken care of it themselves. I sigh, realizing that I've got a lot of growing up to do.

Okay, I need to get back to Adam.

I return to the love seat, where Adam sits, looking bored and grumpy.

His expression shifts back to the suave cool-guy mask when he sees me. "Welcome back, beautiful," he says with a sparkling smile. *Oh yeah, this guy's a real piece of work.* "I'm sorry that took so long. There was a line for the ladies' room." *Stay on top of this, Mel. You need to try with Adam and really consider what Rich said.*

We're sitting at the back of the café, facing the front door, the perfect place to see my parents when they arrive. Thirty minutes of small talk with someone who does little more than talk small. I did this to myself, so I guess trying to work through a conversation with Adam is my punishment for being an idiot.

"You're worth the wait," he says, still working his way through his player handbook.

"Uh-huh. Thanks. So, Adam, what do you do for fun?"

"Um . . . well, I don't know." He pauses, looking confused. "This is all really weird. I mean, I usually just get chicks here and they yap. Girls always go on and on, and I don't have to talk much. Coffee, you know . . . they get all hopped up on caffeine and chatter away. You're different."

A glimpse into the real him . . . interesting. "That's the first honest thing I've heard you say. I'm Melanie, by the way. So, what do you like to do?"

He contemplates the question and visibly relaxes, crossing his leg to rest his ankle on his knee. "Well, I like to work on motorcycles. I rebuilt the one we rode here on, and I've got another one in the garage that's almost roadworthy. I bought it in pieces and spend every spare minute working on it. The whole thing has kind of grown into a business for me. I rebuild motorcycles for clients in my garage."

Now we're talking.

He's toying with the spoon in his coffee cup, looking a bit pensive.

I tilt my head, studying his profile. "I like this side of you a lot better than the whole mysterious hot-guy routine."

He looks at me, surprised. "Really? Girls always seem bored when I talk about what I like. Seemed like the whole brooding, mysterious thing kept their interest, so I went with it." The words tumble out of his mouth, and he looks a little startled by his own admission. He blushes, a charming shade of pink creeping slowly up his neck.

I can't help but smile. "Maybe I'm not like most girls. I don't know much about motorcycles, but I like working with tools. I dig it."

It seems like the real Adam is a little skittish, so I try to make my expression harmless and encouraging. He doesn't react. I wait, wondering what he's thinking. Just when I think I might have read him wrong, he smiles the same genuine smile I saw as we were riding on the canyon.

Looks like there's more to Adam than I thought.

CHAPTER 10

Adam and I relax into a surprisingly great conversation. I'm thinking fast because my parents will be here any minute and I have to figure out how to telegraph to them that Rich was right. Something tells me that Adam hasn't ever been this honest with a girl before. It would be a shame to ruin this breakthrough because I jumped the gun and called my parents.

The café door opens and in walk Mom and Rich, who stop briefly to allow their eyes to adjust to the dim lighting. They make a show of looking nonchalant, talking and laughing. Then they see me and head our way.

"Melanie! What are you doing here?" Mom's face looks strained with the effort not to break character.

My stepfather stands with his arms crossed over his chest as he surveys Adam.

"Mom!" I say, acting surprised. "Rich. What are *you* doing here?"

Before any more can be said, Adam leaps up from the couch and stretches out his hand to Rich. "Melanie's parents! It's so nice to meet you. I'm Adam, and this is my fault. Please don't be mad at her. I'm really sorry."

Mom and Rich look from Adam, to me, and then at each other.

"Sounds like you two have had an interesting day," Mom says.

Rich shakes his head, looking like he's at war between trying to appear angry and trying not to laugh. "That your Harley out front?" He juts his thumb over his shoulder toward the door.

Adam nods, looking a little sheepish.

"Nice bike, son. I don't know what the hell's happening, but the coffee smells good, and I see cheesecake in that case. How about you two let us order something, and we can all chat for a bit?"

Adam exhales and his shoulders relax. "That sounds good." He guides me back to the love seat.

We settle in while Mom and Rich order coffee and pastries. We don't speak another word until they return and sit in the armchairs across from us.

"How long have you been riding Harleys?" Rich asks, genuine interest playing across his sharp features.

"I've been riding for two years, but my dad taught me how to build motorcycles when I was ten. I want to be a mechanic. I build Harleys from parts in my garage. Didn't intend for it to become a business, but word got around and it just kind of happened. I love hunting for parts at salvage yards, and clients started coming to me through word of mouth. I built the one out front."

"Then we should talk shop sometime. I'm an old-time Harley lover." Rich pauses, his expression growing serious, and switching gears. "You two want to explain why you're here instead of school?"

Again, Adam beats me to it. "This is the part where I'd normally try to talk my way out, but Melanie seems to prefer my honest side, so I'll give it to you straight."

Rich and Mom exchange a smirk.

"We weren't born yesterday," Rich says. "I highly recommend that you lean toward the most honest version possible."

"Yes, sir," Adam says. He leans forward in his seat. "Well, Melanie and I met the other day at . . . lunch."

He glances sideways at me, realizing he almost slipped about Smokers' Corner. I give him the slightest smile before averting my eyes.

"So, today, when I decided to ditch school . . ." He pauses, flustered. "Sir and ma'am, I'll work on that. I should probably stick around at school a little longer each day." He sighs with the realization that he isn't giving the best impression.

Rich seems to take pity on him. "I ditched a few times in my day. Keep going. You haven't blown it so far."

A relieved grin flashes on Adam's face, and he turns to me. "I was getting ready to leave, but I thought about Melanie before I headed out. I know where she has lunch, and I figured I should rescue her. Correct me if I'm wrong, Mel, but you'd been harassed all day. It was kind of funny at first, but after a while"—he returns his attention to Mom and Rich—"she looked really miserable. I thought she could use a break, so I went to get her. I'm not a big talker. Well, usually, I'm not. I didn't really know what to say to her, but she came with me anyway." He sputters to a stop, staring at my parents' confused faces.

Mom's expression projects worry, and she turns to me. "Why were you being harassed?"

They don't know about the nominations!

"Long story short, homecoming nominations were today. I didn't think much of it. I nominated Presley and Marcus. But when we got the results, my name was on the ballot. Now every guy I've never met at school has asked me to the dance. I could barely even get to class. It was like a damn obstacle course." I turn to Adam. "I didn't know you'd noticed."

"Yeah, I noticed. I was in the hall when Dirk came up to you. I couldn't help but watch that show." He laughs and rubs his eyes. "I knew before he asked you that he'd get shot down. Even I think that guy's gross, and I spend most of my time covered in motorcycle grease. Then Joel stopped you, and I decided that I better keep an eye out. Mel, Joel's dangerous. I've known that dude for years. He has a past." His energy shifts to something that seems almost menacing. Then he softens and turns to Mom and Rich. "I'm serious about that. She needs to stay away from him."

Rich nods, an unspoken message passing between them like a conspiracy.

I'll take it. I've decided that I like Adam, and if he can get on my parents' good side, that's half the battle.

Adam clears his throat and glances at me. "About all the dance invites . . ." He hesitates, looking down. "I overheard a rumor that you need to know about, Melanie."

My eyebrows furrow and I side-eye my parents, who are leaning forward in their seats. "Okay. That doesn't sound good. What is it?"

Adam, radiating discomfort, rubs his thumb on his forehead. "For the record, I'm not usually one to pay attention to gossip, but this one I couldn't help but overhear. All those dance invites you've been getting are the result of a plan orchestrated by Victoria and her pack of hyenas."

My face scrunches up. "What do you mean?"

Adam looks down at his hands. "Victoria and company have been spreading a rumor around school that you're 'easy and sleazy.' They're doing it because they want the school's bottom-feeder jackasses to ask you to the dance." He looks up, meeting my eyes. "I'm sorry, Mel. I know that's not who you are. And to be honest, I thought if it got around school that you left with me at lunch, it might curb the rumors." He glances at Rich. "I've got a reputation at the school as a bruiser. Most of those guys will likely back off if they think she's with me."

I sigh, tipping my head back. "I'm an idiot. I should've known something was up."

Mom rubs her temples. "Victoria strikes again." She glances at me. "What's your plan, Mel?"

"Leave Victoria to me," Adam offers, a devious expression on his face. "You might have noticed that she's into me. She's been chasing after me like a heifer in heat since the first day of school."

I crack up. "Deal. But make sure I'm there. I don't want to miss this show."

Mom and Rich both laugh.

"I like you, Adam," Rich says.

Suddenly Mom's eyes are sparkling with excitement. "So . . . are you homecoming princess?"

I sag with exhaustion. "We find out on Monday."

"Adam, do you go to the dances?" Mom asks this with a lilt to her tone that makes me instantly turn red.

Of course, I secretly hoped he would ask me, but since it didn't come up while we were talking, I figured I'd read him wrong.

He looks amused by the question and not the least bit uncomfortable. At least I don't have to kill my mom for humiliating me.

"I avoid the dances," Adam says. "Dressing up in a penguin suit and doing the Roger Rabbit in a room full of sweaty idiots isn't really my bag. No offense, Mel. It's not that I don't want to go with you. It's just that it's the kind of social headache I dread. I'm sure someone who isn't so bad will ask you."

Sigh. Hope deflates. I glance at Mom, who is also clearly disappointed.

"Thank you for your honesty, Adam," she says, rallying. "We still have a thousand questions, but I think we have an idea of what's happening. On a different note, Mel, we have a dance dress to shop for."

This surprises me. Mom usually hates shopping. It's like all this princess nomination news has ignited the teen girl in her.

"Do you think I should even go to the dance?" I ask hesitantly.

Rich gives me his "you have to be kidding" look. "You're going to this dance, Mel. I'm not about to let you miss out on high-school fun just because this Victoria girl is jealous."

I consider this for a moment before breaking into a grin. "You're right. Mom, let's go shopping."

All at once, we're standing and Rich is talking about how we should hurry if we want to beat traffic. He rushes to stack the empty dishes neatly on the end table, then takes Mom by the hand and motions for me to join them.

"Sir," Adam says, rising, "if it's okay, I'd like to take Melanie back to school. We should get there just before the final bell."

"Why?" Mom asks.

"I'm going to confront Victoria," Adam explains.

Rich, clearly amused, looks from Mom to me. "Well, Adam, I guess that'd be all right." He leans in and smiles at me. "I can't wait to hear all about it when you get home."

"Game on, Mel," Adam says with a sneering smile. "Let's go teach Victoria a lesson."

CHAPTER 11

Adam pulls into the faculty parking lot, and I get off the motorcycle.

"Walk over to the bus road and follow my lead when I talk to Victoria," Adam says. "I'll see you over there."

I nod, grinning with anticipation, as Adam pulls out of the parking lot. I hightail it through Actors' Alley just as the last bell of the day rings. Presley and Marcus see me and rush down the staircase, jogging to catch up.

"How did it go with the monster?" Presley asks.

"Surprisingly well, actually," I say with a grin.

Presley looks sheepish. "That's good. Listen, Mel. There's something you should know. It's about Victoria."

I cut her off with a wave of my hand. "I already heard about it. She's about to get what she deserves. Just wait for it."

Presley and Marcus exchange a look, but we arrive at the bus road before she can ask me anything else. Adam's leaning on his Harley in the alley driveway. He's situated in the perfect place where everyone on the bus road and in the alley can see him. He pretends to ignore me as my friends and I come to a stop about twenty feet away.

"He's got a plan," I whisper to Presley and Marcus.

There's a gleam in their eyes.

We all wait.

The moment Victoria rounds the corner into the alley, Adam calls out to her. "Hey, Victoria, come here!"

Victoria looks surprised before quickly recovering. She runs her fingers through her hair and not so subtly gives her shirt a quick yank to reveal more cleavage. She whispers something to her snotty friends before picking up the pace, her hips swerving so dramatically it's impressive she doesn't tip over.

Presley snorts. "Do guys actually find that trash sexy?" she asks Marcus.

Marcus rolls his eyes and passes her the huge bag of M&M's that has materialized from his backpack. "We need snacks for this show."

When Victoria gets to Adam, she runs her finger along the side of his Harley's handlebars. Then she looks up at him coyly through her lashes. "What's up?"

Adam smiles flirtatiously. "I've been thinking about you." His loud, commanding voice attracts the attention of everyone in the area, delivering him the audience he's aiming for.

"Oh yeah?" Victoria says. "What have you been thinking?" She rolls her shoulders seductively.

With a grin, Adam lifts Victoria and sets her sidesaddle on the motorcycle. She swoons as he starts strutting through the growing crowd. I watch him and then catch the eye of Victoria's hallway guy, who is standing about ten feet away, looking pensive.

Adam turns to Victoria. "I was thinking you'd be the perfect girl to ask to the homecoming dance. But first, you have to pass a test. Think you can do it?"

Victoria gives him a come-hither look. She tosses her perfect hair over her shoulder and purrs, "Hit me with it."

"First question . . . ," Adam says with theatrical flair. "Can you look hot enough to be my date?"

Everyone snaps their heads to Victoria, waiting for her answer. She extends her tan, slender leg. "Duh! Have you seen me?"

"Of course, of course," Adam says with a nod. "Silly me. Just look at you! Smokin' hot, right?"

She shrugs, smiling coyly.

"Second question, but this one is for the audience. You see, I only like nice girls." He scans the crowd. "How many of you think Victoria is a nice girl?"

Only the Drones, huddled in a clump a few feet from Victoria's hallway guy, raise their hands. They glance around, surprised, seemingly, to discover not everyone worships Victoria.

I can't help but smirk.

Adam looks over-the-top baffled. "That can't be!" He looks Victoria's way. "Surely there must be a mistake." He pretends to ponder for a moment before adding, "Let's try this another way. How many of you has Victoria been nasty to?"

The crowd freezes. After an uncomfortable moment of silence, dozens of people tentatively raise their hands. By the time it's over, nearly every hand is up.

Victoria, glancing around the crowd, seems confused. Then her face falls, and she looks like she might cry.

Adam pretends to reassure her. "Aw, Victoria. What happened to the sexy pose? You look so hot on the Harley." He straightens and his expression hardens. "Okay, okay . . . question three, and this is a big one. You see, I don't like drama." He points at her. "So,

Victoria, are you willing to apologize for being a batshit crazy, jealous, shallow, bitchy, rude *gossip*?"

The crowd collectively holds their breath. All eyes are on Victoria, whose face has turned tomato red, looking as if she might die of shame.

When she says nothing, Adam addresses the crowd. "As most of you know, since the ballots for homecoming royalty came out, this maniacal bitch has been spreading a rumor about Melanie Slate, calling Melanie 'easy and sleazy.' I personally find that hilarious, considering that's how many people would describe Victoria."

Everyone laughs, except for Joel, who catches my eye from the other side of the crowd. Once again, he's hyper focused on me and only diverts his attention to glare at Adam momentarily before snapping his laser gaze back to me.

Adam continues his speech, dragging me back to reality.

"But I digress . . . ," he says. "I'd like to help put these rumors to rest, so here goes. First, I'd like to assure you all that Melanie's a nice girl and not the least bit sleazy *or* easy. Some of you fell for the rumors because you asked yourselves, 'Why would Victoria make up things about Melanie and not Presley, who's also her competition on the ballot?' I'll tell you why. Presley over here"—Adam, grinning, gestures to Presley—"is a beast, who doesn't take shit from anyone. She would gleefully kick Victoria's ass in front of the entire school and doesn't give a damn if she gets suspended."

"Truth!" Presley calls out. "Screw you, Victoria!"

This brings another round of laughter. I glance across to Victoria's hallway guy, who seems to be growing more and more uncomfortable.

"So, you see," Adam continues, "Victoria knew better than to mess with Presley because, believe it or not, Victoria isn't as stupid as she looks. Bullies rarely enjoy a challenge, and Presley would definitely present a challenge. For any of you who have yet to figure it out, Jiggle Wiggle Fun over here"—he gestures to Victoria—"is one of the biggest bullies at this school." Adam pauses to stare her down for a moment. "Back to the matter at hand. Victoria has had it in for Melanie for a while now, and I'm guessing it's because she's threatened by her." He stalks to Victoria's side and turns to face the crowd. "I'm here to tell you that Victoria's a pathetic sludge stain. You're welcome to talk all the shit you want about her, and no one who matters is gonna care. What *will* stop is the gossip about Melanie. Any guy caught gossiping about Melanie will have to deal with me . . . personally."

The crowd breaks into wild applause.

Adam takes a bow before shooing a crimson-faced Victoria off his motorcycle. "Hoof it to the buses."

Victoria, thoroughly humiliated, slides down and attempts to cross the crowd to hallway guy, who skirts around her and keeps walking. She's left with only her Drones, who are now visibly ashamed to be seen with her.

Adam turns toward me and crosses the distance between us. He runs his finger along my jaw, and before I know what's happening, he kisses me in front of everyone. My breath catches, and I melt. The whole crowd is watching my first kiss, but I manage to play it cool.

He hesitantly ends the kiss and then grins. "See you later, Mel." He returns to his Harley and swings his leg over the seat. Effortlessly, he fires up the engine and takes off, speeding out of sight.

I turn, dazed, to find Presley and Marcus looking gleeful.

I grin back at them, eyes wide.

"Call me after auditions tonight," Presley says. "We've *got* to talk."

As I head through the now thinning crowd, I notice Joel is still there. He's the only one not moving. He hits me with a narrow-eyed stare that radiates malice.

CHAPTER *12*

Auditions were everything!

I grin to myself. I've got some work to do, and I might not make this show cast, but I know what I need to do to be ready when the next chance presents itself. I round the corner, exiting the alley just as the last activities bus turns right onto Highland.

Damn it!

Mr. Isley held me for callbacks, which ran late. I should have let him know I needed to catch the bus. Exhausted and frustrated, I close my eyes. *Better call Mom.* I heft my backpack onto my other shoulder and trudge all the way across campus to the pay phones on the backside of the Commons.

Fishing quarters out of the bottom of my pack proves a chore, but I finally come up with a few. I dial home and wait impatiently while it rings. Nervous energy creeps up my spine, and I feel my intuition spark. The campus looks different this close to dark, and my eyes dart one way and then the other, but it appears I'm alone. On the fifth ring, the answering machine picks up. My head tips back and my eyes close.

What do I do now?

With a roll of my eyes, I riffle around in the front pouch of my pack for the little slip of paper that Adam wrote his phone number on. I hesitantly drop another quarter into the pay phone and dial.

Adam picks up on the second ring. "Hello?"

"Hi, it's Melanie."

I can practically hear him smiling as he says, "Hey, Mel. What's up?"

"I'm sorry to bother you with this, but Mr. Isley held me for callbacks, the late buses already left, and I can't get hold of my mom."

"Where are you?" Adam's voice holds a touch of worry.

"At school. I know you're busy, but—"

I'm distracted by movement to my right and gasp as a sudden roar of intuitive energy surges through me.

Whatever's about to happen, it's going to be bad.

"Melanie," Adam says, "what's wrong?"

Before I can answer, Joel rounds the corner of the athletics building across the way. I inhale sharply as my intuition nearly doubles me over. My brain sputters before terror rips away all sensibility. Joel is radiating violence, with an edge of sick seduction.

Adam asks again, his voice strained this time, "What's *wrong?*"

With a quavering voice, I answer, "Joel. Hurry."

"Run, Melanie! I'll be there in ten minutes."

Fear coils up my spine, and the phone slips from my hand. Joel is standing, statue still, roughly twenty feet away. When his face splits with a sadistic grin, I know I'm in serious trouble.

On the verge of panic, I catch myself before my knees nearly buckle.

Joel whistles, and the tune is eerily familiar, though I can't place it. He singsongs, "Mel-an-ie" and then whistles the tune again. I realize it's the beginning cadence of "Janie's Got a Gun."

Creep!

"You're a brazen little bitch, aren't you?" Joel says. "All alone on campus in the dark."

My heart pounds, but I don't respond. *What do I do now?*

Making the decision for me, Joel sprints in my direction. I take off and run as fast as I can around the Commons building. Joel's feet are pounding the pavement right behind me, and I feel a rush of evil energy just before he tackles me.

My face and shoulder skid on the pavement. I see stars.

Joel's on top of me, but my backpack's in his way. He pulls it off with a brutal yank to the right, wrenching my shoulder. When I scream, he clamps his hand over my mouth. He grabs my arm and twists me around to face him, my back raking against the concrete. I claw at his face, making gashes with my fingernails. I struggle to fight back, but he gets me pinned under him.

Trapped under Joel's weight, I'm panting, wide-eyed as he stares down at me exuding the evilest energy I've ever felt. He jams his knee into my pelvis and presses hard, holding me down while he gets my tank top in both hands and rips it open. I'm completely trapped under the weight of him, and there's nothing I can do but scream. I let loose with a cacophony of sound.

Joel clamps a hand over my mouth, and I knee him hard in the crotch. He doubles over and I roll, trying to get my feet under me. He grabs me around the waist and slams me down hard on my back, knocking the air out of me.

He leans down and sneers. "Shut up, or I'll knock your ass out. We're doing this either way, but I prefer you awake. The terror in your eyes is what's going to do it for me."

My brain tornados as his words sink in and I realize that there's nothing I can do to stop him. *If I live through this, I'm going to learn how to defend myself better,* I vow to myself as tears roll down my cheeks and land on his hand. He takes his hand away from my mouth and licks my tears off his finger while he glowers at me. The heat in his expression is the scariest thing I've ever seen.

He grabs my wrists, slithering down on top of me. My intuition flares to life, my chest seizes with crushing pain, and suddenly I know what makes Joel tick. Obsession. Adam kissed me and now Joel's more obsessed than ever.

I'm petrified to the point that I can't make sound. I'm on the verge of passing out when I hear Adam's Harley rev in the distance.

Joel's head snaps up and is lit by the stream of the Harley's headlight shining from nearby. "This isn't over," he hisses at me. "I'll be back for you." He leans over and licks the side of my face from chin to temple before pushing himself hard off my body.

It knocks the wind out of me for a second time, and I roll onto my side, gasping for air.

Joel steps around and, with a malicious smile, kicks me in the stomach at full force. Pain explodes in my gut. I watch as he takes off running, rounding the two-story building toward the teachers' parking lot.

Adam screeches to a halt a few feet away. The engine idles, and I hear his feet hit the ground when he jumps off the bike.

He kneels next to me. "Melanie, are you okay?"

I shake my head, unable to speak from the fear and stomach pain. He picks me up, cradling me, and I rest my head on his chest. Tears roll down my face.

Adam waits while I relearn how to breathe.

Finally, when my hands stop shaking, he asks, "Can I put you down so I can look you over?"

I nod, and he sets me down and turns me to look at my back. He turns me back to face him and finishes checking me over. "You have road rash on your face and shoulder. Anything else I've missed?"

I nod, unable to speak, and take his hand, putting it on my stomach where a giant bruise is already developing. The spot is hot to the touch.

"That's going to hurt tomorrow," he says.

Finally, I'm able to speak. "He was going to rape me."

Adam snarls and glances around, searching for Joel.

It suddenly occurs to me that I'm standing here in only a bra, my torn tank top discarded on the pavement below. I cross my arms over my chest, doing little to cover anything. Adam looks down the second he notices.

He tips my chin up and says, "I know you just met me, but you standing here in a bra is the last thing you need to be worried about right now. You can trust me." He drapes his jacket over the motorcycle seat and pulls off his tank top. "Arms up."

I start to lift my arms, and an irrational giggle bubbles up.

Adam stops midmotion, looking confused. He tilts his head. "Tell me what you're thinking."

I laugh a little. "First, I was thinking, 'He's about to dress me like a toddler.' Then I thought, 'My usual post-trauma hysteria strikes again. If he wasn't done with me already, after all this drama, he will be when he realizes I'm quirky.'"

A surprised laugh belts from Adam. He wraps his arms around me and pulls me in for a hug. "I like you, Melanie. You surprise me."

Both of us shirtless and pressed together makes me gasp as my brain practically leaks out my ears. He looks down at me, and suddenly I can't stop the heat emanating from my expression, the post-battle adrenaline making a sharp shift into something new. Adam looks at me quizzically at first, before his expression shifts to match my heat. His breath catches, and his hand slides to the side of my neck. When he leans down and kisses me lightly, my mind tornadoes.

He pulls away and stares down at me while I catch my breath.

"Your pupils are dilated," he says. "You're in shock. Don't make any big decisions right now. You need to clear your head."

I look down, my heart pounding.

"There's somewhere I want to take you," he says. "You can fill me in on what happened. Are you game?"

I nod.

"Okay. Arms up."

I raise my arms, and he slides his tank down over me.

"It's too big," I say. "It doesn't cover much."

He smiles. "True, but it's more about you feeling safe than anything else."

"What about Joel?"

"I'll deal with him later."

He puts his jacket back on, swings his leg over the bike, and reaches his hand out to help me on behind him. The engine revs, and suddenly we're flying through the school toward the exit gate.

CHAPTER 13

When Adam kills the Harley's engine, sudden quiet envelopes us. I slide off the back and clear space for Adam. The night air is perfect, the moon hanging low in the sky, as I turn and stare out at the city lights below the overlook. It feels as if we're the only two people on the planet. Adam touches my hand, and I turn to him. He pulls me to him, picks me up, and sits me down facing him on the front half of the seat. I smile and wrap my legs around his waist, leaning back with my head on the handlebars. His arms settle on my legs.

"How far did Joel get?" he asks quietly.

I shake my head. "Ripped my shirt off. Told me to shut up because he wants to get off on the terror in my eyes while he rapes me." I shiver. "He licked my tears off his fingers."

Adam's winces. "Damn. I thought I was bent. Are you okay?"

I shake my head. "I need to learn to defend myself because you can bet your ass that what just happened will *never* happen again." I sigh. "Considering that I've never been shirtless with a guy before Joel, I'm definitely not okay. I'm not as weak as I come across, though."

Adam regards me curiously. "Can I ask you something personal?"

I nod.

"You've never been shirtless with a guy. How many boyfriends have you had?"

I'm nervous and look up at the moon. "None."

Adam tips back his head and closes his eyes before leveling me with a serious expression. "We'll figure out what to do about Joel. I'm sorry, Melanie. Given this new information, would you rather not sit like this?"

I consider my options for a moment. "Do you want the real answer, or am I supposed to make up some coy bullshit that sounds proper?"

He laughs. "I don't know how you do it, but you keep surprising me. I always prefer honesty—brutal or otherwise."

I smile and nod. "No. I don't want to move. I'm happy exactly how things are right now." I glance to the side. "I'm having a damn hard time not thinking of you shirtless under that jacket, but I'm enjoying this."

"I date a lot, but I don't usually enjoy the company. You're different."

I raise an eyebrow and sit up, joking, "Is that one of your go-to lines with the Missies?"

He laughs again. "No, Little Miss Snarky. It's not."

When I giggle, he pulls me closer. I slide my arms around his neck, and he kisses me. My heart beats hard, my chest against his chest. He chuckles, pulling away.

"What's so funny?" I ask.

"You are. The pounding heart—hormones or fear?"

I grin. "Hormones. I'm not scared of you."

He tips my chin up. "Perfect." He kisses me again, and I nearly melt.

He leaves me breathless, my eyes unfocused, as he pulls away this time. We sit there flustered for a time before collecting ourselves.

"I knew there was something wrong before I even called you," I say. "I ignored it. I feel like an idiot. I've had this sense of intuition so long that you think I'd know better." Too late, I realize that I've just filled Adam in on my deepest personal secret, and I don't even really know him.

He looks at me, curiosity brightening his expression. "I'm intrigued. Tell me more."

"Sorry," I say with a shake of my head. "I don't usually hit people with something that heavy right after I meet them."

"I'm glad you did."

I shrug. "All right, but it might send you running."

He glances to the side with a contemplative look before meeting my gaze. "I'm a lot more intrigued by you than I expected to be. Being totally honest, I don't think anything you're about to say is going to do anything but make me more interested."

It takes me a minute to calm my nerves to the point where I can tell him the rest of my secret. "I have a wicked accurate sense of intuition. It sounds like science fiction, and no one but my parents ever believes me, so I never discuss it. It boils down to this: I know things are going to happen before they do. I can't remember the last time it was wrong. Tonight it fired up when I got to the pay phones, and I ignored it."

"How does it work?"

I ponder the question. "It's hard to explain, but I get an almost painful feeling here." I put my hand on his chest. "I usually have an idea of who it's about and how bad whatever it is will be. It's come in handy."

He contemplates what I've just told him, the silence extending right up to the point where I start worrying that I've completely freaked him out. Finally, he asks, "How often does your intuition fire up?"

"Interesting question," I say. "So far, it tends to fire up in two ways. Either when something life-or-death bad happens and I need to immediately get out of danger, or when my life is changing dramatically because of something huge that's about to happen."

He nods and smiles the slightest bit. Then his eyes narrow thoughtfully, and my heart beats a little harder.

He's gorgeous when he gets lost in thought.

"How much control do you have of it?" he asks.

"Literally almost none. It pops up without much doing on my part. I've learned to listen to it, though."

"Here, let me show you something. It sounds like you might not know about it yet." He takes my hand. "You feel that energy?"

I nod.

"You do realize you're what's called an energy worker, right? It's likely how this intuition of yours works. You also must have a touch of a psychic gift."

When I look at him quizzically, he laughs.

"You've made it this far and don't know that?"

I shake my head. "Fifteen years, and I've never heard of any of this."

He looks suddenly unsure. "Fifteen, huh? That's questionable. I'm playing with fire with you."

"How old are you?"

"Seventeen, nearly eighteen."

I shrug. "It's legal. We're good."

He laughs. "Okay. Here's the deal. You need to learn how to ground out your energy. Put your hands in mine and close your eyes. I'm going to let my energy loose. I'm hiding a lot."

I take his hands, close my eyes, and focus. I feel the gentle radiation coming from his hands before the energy suddenly shifts. It thrums through my hands with an edge of manic seduction. I gasp and snap my eyes open.

"That's what's actually going on in me," he says, grinning. "You've got me a little spun out."

I smirk flirtatiously at him.

When he laughs, the energy thrums harder from his hands. He shakes his head, clearly interested, and breathes, "Damn, girl. You're trouble." After a moment of contemplative silence, he returns us to the lesson. "Now, focus again."

I close my eyes, and, after a moment, his energy shifts to a calm hum. I look back up at him, surprise radiating from me. "Explain how you did that."

"I'll try, but I don't usually teach this stuff. Soon, I'll introduce you to my two friends who taught me all this." He pauses. "I want you to think of it like your energy is water and the earth is a sponge. You need to channel the energy down and let it absorb into the earth."

I close my eyes and focus inward, concentrating. It's a struggle at first, but then something clicks in me. I feel the energy channel down and release out like an internal exhale.

With a gasp, my eyes fly open.

Adam is grinning at me. "Hell, yes! That was perfect."

Suddenly, all the anxiety I live with on a daily basis is gone. My brain sputters, trying to comprehend the shift, and for a time I'm lost in thought. After a long silence, I gaze up at Adam and say with an edge of wonderment, "I've lived with crippling anxiety my entire life. That just fixed it."

He smiles softly at me.

"Thank you," I say. "You have no idea."

His expression softens around the edges, and he stares at me for a long moment before saying, "I really like you." Pensively, he looks to the side, his mood shifting. "I've got a reputation that you've likely already heard about from your friends."

When I nod, he breaks into the slightest smirk.

"Please know that I'm not using you," he says. "I'm genuinely interested."

I melt into his ocean blue eyes. Unsure what to say, but positive about what I feel, I put my hands flat on his chest and slide them around his back, under the jacket. He closes his eyes, and his energy becomes an erratic, seductive throb. I smile to myself and kiss his neck lightly. He shivers and tips his head down, his lips meeting mine.

CHAPTER 14

When we hear Adam's Harley rumble up to the curb, Mom suddenly looks worried.

"You sure about this guy?" she asks. "He's a little old for you."

"You liked him when you met him," I say with a shrug. "And he helped me after the attack."

Mom gently grips my chin and tilts my head to the side, surveying the angry road rash covering half of my face and shoulder. "I'm starting to think this school is a bad idea."

"I'm not leaving the school, Mom," I tell her with a shake of my head. "I finally have friends. In a matter of weeks, I've gone from being a nobody to being on the homecoming court ballot. I'm not running from this."

Mom sighs. "I almost miss the quiet wallflower you were in junior high."

"Well, I don't miss her. This version of me is who I really am. Even though this whole situation with Joel, Victoria, and the Drones is insane, I feel like I can finally breathe."

We're interrupted by the doorbell. Mom opens the door, and Adam strides through with a wide grin.

"Good to see you again, Carol," he says.

Mom seems to soften a little as she greets him, Adam's charm burning through a bit of her protective instinct.

"I know ditching school doesn't sound like the responsible plan," Adam says sheepishly, "but I think a day to recoup might be good for her. I was hoping Mel and I could have a chill day."

Mom considers this, while I hold my breath, wondering what she's going to say. My parents are strict about school, but I find myself loving Adam's unexpected suggestion.

Finally, Mom sighs. "As much as I hate for her to miss school, I have to admit that I'm nervous about the idea of her going today." She appraises Adam. "You'll drive carefully?"

He nods.

She glances from him to me. "No funny business," she says bluntly. "Got it?"

A blush creeps up my neck. "Dang, Mom. Way to cut to the chase."

Mom and I glance at Adam, who radiates amusement.

"You have my word that there will be no funny business," he says.

Mom and I crack up as Adam glances to the side, chuckling quietly.

"I thought we'd go to Third Street Promenade and hang out," he says.

My excitement bubbles over. "Please, Mom! I could use a shopping spree to work on my boring wardrobe." I clasp my hands in front of me and wiggle a little, excited.

Mom rolls her eyes. Then she grins and opens our silverware drawer, where she keeps her envelope of mad money. She pulls out a collection of bills and hands them to me. "I can't believe I'm agreeing to this," she says under her breath.

With a squeal, I bounce in to hug her. Adam has to call back over his shoulder to thank her, as I shuttle him out the door before she can change her mind. We jog down the red-brick front walkway and hop on his Harley.

Just before he takes off, I wrap my arms around him and grin.

The ride to Santa Monica is beautiful but long. My sore muscles move slow as I climb off the bike. Adam turns to me and, like my mom earlier, tilts my chin to the side and examines the damage from Joel's attack. He gestures to my stomach, and I lift my shirt so he can see the giant bruise. He winces and shakes his head, seemingly lost in his own thoughts. After a contemplative moment, he perks up, throwing an arm around my shoulder.

We walk around the corner, where the magic of Third Street Promenade opens before us. I haven't been here in years, but it's just as I remembered. Street musicians, singers, hip-hop dancers, artists from all walks are spread out here and there. The street is barricaded by giant planters at each intersection, making it a traffic-free shopping center.

We amble down the road until Adam stops in front of a street musician playing a haunting acoustic rendition of "Hotel California." After Adam drops a folded bill in the guy's open guitar case, he turns to me, bows comically, and offers his hand. I laugh, taking it, and he spins me against him before spinning me back out, our arms stretched. He smirks seductively and draws me into a slow dance.

"I'm not usually into spending actual quality time with girls," he admits.

I tilt my head. "But this is somehow different?"

He nods and chuckles a bit. "I'm usually a little quicker with the funny business your mom made me swear off."

I stop dancing, rise onto the balls of my feet, and wrap my arms around his neck. He leans in and kisses me, and the whole world slides away. There's a fire in his kiss that sends my head spinning. My knees turn to Jell-O. He picks me up and holds me against him.

I really like this guy.

"Where to, Mel?" he asks as he sets me down. "This is your day."

"Think we can hit some of the shops?" I ask a little shyly. "I feel like most of my clothes aren't really appropriate for our school."

Adam grins. "Hell, yes! I've got you. I know exactly where to go."

I step out of the dressing room in the outfit Adam selected for me.

He nods, saying, "Damn! That'll work," as I turn to survey myself in the mirror.

Skintight black shimmer leggings, and a red slouch top, strategically cut to peek-a-boo one black bra strap. I smile, slow and wicked, before turning to Adam and raising an eyebrow.

He laughs and steps up to me, his expression morphing seductively as he picks me up and slides into the dressing room before anyone can notice. He closes the door behind us and sets me down.

Adam puts a hand flat on my sternum while purposefully guiding me back until my shoulders rest against the wall. He places one hand on the wall above my shoulder and leans in, kissing my neck, while pulling my hips to him. I gasp and close my eyes. Energy flares between us, and we both sharply inhale.

"You're definitely trouble, all right," Adam whispers in my ear. "But your mom said, 'No funny business.'"

"There's nothing funny about this business," I purr, "so we're good."

Adam's mouth drops open. Clearly enjoying my suggestive comeback.

I peer at him through my lashes and slide my hands under his jacket, slowly running them around his sides to rest on his back. His eyes close. I lightly run my nails from his shoulders to his waist.

He turns his head, his expression almost pained. "I know I started this," he mumbles, his voice deep and gravelly, "but you're taking it to a place I might not have the willpower to stop."

I whisper back, "Then let's make this interesting."

He takes a gasping breath and opens his eyes, leveling me with a look weighted in seductive curiosity.

I smile coyly, knowing I'm playing with fire yet choosing not to care.

I hop up, wrapping my legs around his waist, and he catches me.

He bites his lip and his eyebrows furrow.

"Hang on to that resolve, Adam," I say. "I love a good game."

His expression is laced with the love of a challenge. I kiss his neck, featherlight, mimicking his flirtation from a moment ago. When he gasps, I meet his nearly tortured blue-eyed gaze.

I lean in until our lips are almost touching. "Don't do it, Adam," I whisper, smiling against his lips. "Hold out."

Our breathing becomes ragged, and the rise and fall of my chest against his makes him shiver as he fights the instinct to kiss me. Just when the anticipation reaches a quaking point, I kiss him. Fire shoots up both of our spines, and he catches himself on the wall with one arm as his knees go weak. His grip on me loosens, and I squeeze my legs tighter around him, trying to keep myself from falling. He steadies himself and presses my back to the wall, taking the kiss to a fiery new level.

He ends the kiss and leaves me panting.

His eyes are unfocused, and he rattles his head to restore sense to his throttling mind. I watch him with an amused half smile.

When he can comprehend reality again, he asks, "You said you're fifteen?"

I giggle and chirp girlishly, "Yup. No clue where that came from. You bring out my inner wild child, I guess."

"I'll keep that in mind," he jokes, setting me down.

I laugh and pull off the shirt, returning it to its hanger.

"Would you like me to leave?" Adam asks, amused.

I glance over my shoulder. "Not particularly. We're having a nice chat."

He smirks, apparently surprised by my answer, and backs up a few steps to lean against the opposite wall. "All right," he says quietly. "But I plan to enjoy the view, and I'm not going to apologize for it."

I slide off the leggings and hang them up. "I was hoping you'd say that."

He studies me appreciatively as I turn, wearing only my black bra and underwear, and begin to dress. His expression is riddled with an odd combination of shock and amorous interest that I thoroughly enjoy.

Once dressed, I slip my feet into my sandals and straighten. Then I cross to him and ask demurely, "You okay?"

He blinks rapidly. "Damn, Firecracker. Way to screw with a guy's head. I think I may have met my match."

I allow the attraction I've barely got control of to slip behind my eyes again. "There's something about you. . ." I rise on my toes and kiss him again.

He melts.

— —

We come to a stop on the pier down the road from the shopping center. I set down my bags and lean against the railing, looking out at the ocean. Adam steps up behind and rests his hands on the railing on either side of me. The breeze, the sound of the waves, the scent of him—I close my eyes in contentment.

"Tell me what you're thinking," he says.

"I was just thinking that, until now, I've never felt like I belonged in California. Like the fun and sparkle of this state just weren't for me, or something. As terrible as last night was, the rest of my time at Hollywood High has opened up a whole new world I've always longed to be a part of."

I look back out at the waves as Adam sits on the railing next to me.

"You're the oddest combination of bold and shy," he says. "I like how you think."

I regard him curiously. "I've never thought of myself that way," I confess. "Thank you."

He smiles. "So we've successfully managed to avoid school for a day. Do you think you can handle it tomorrow?"

"I'm not as fragile as I come across. I can deal with Joel."

Adam is lost in thought for a moment, then says, "I'm starting to see how well you can handle yourself. But, Melanie, everyone in that group of Joel's is just as bad as he is." He meets my gaze. "Please let me help you. The things he's done go well beyond you. You aren't the first girl he's hurt."

When I start to protest, he silences me with a reassuring gaze.

"I'm not going to deal with him alone. There are several guys at school I plan to talk to. Will you be okay if we step in on your behalf?"

I think about this for a second, not liking any of it. "I don't want to be treated like a porcelain doll."

Adam shakes his head, and he smirks as if recalling our dressing room encounter. "I don't think of you that way at all."

Protest flashes in my mind again. Finally, I sigh. "Just make sure I'm there when you deal with him."

"Deal." He smiles. "Oh, I almost forgot. You need a working stone." He digs into his jacket pocket and pulls out a gorgeous clear quartz crystal hanging from a long, delicate chain. He dangles it in front of me. "This caught my eye. I bought it for you while you were busy trying on clothes."

My mouth drops open, and I breathe, "Did you, really?"

He nods, and I reach out to touch the shimmering pendant.

My gaze shifts to Adam's. "Thank you," I say sincerely. "I love it."

He hops down from the railing and slips the necklace over my head, leaving it to rest on my chest. "You're welcome." He turns me around and backs me against the railing, gliding his thumb along my jaw before leaning in to kiss me.

CHAPTER 15

I get off the bus, and Adam is waiting. He pushes away from the wall and stalks my way, radiating aggression.

I've been a nervous wreck the entire bus ride.

He reaches me and meets my gaze, smiling just the slightest bit before pulling me in for a hug. "Ground it out, Melanie. We're going to go deal with Joel, and you're blasting nervous energy. Joel's intuitive, too, and he'll take it as a challenge."

I nod, my cheek against Adam's chest, and close my eyes. I focus inward like he taught me, gathering the erratic energy and channeling it down and out. I feel Adam nod against the top of my head.

"Damn, you learn fast. You've already got this down." He tips my chin up, looking me in the eyes. "You're remarkable." When he kisses me, the rush of students disappears, and I'm swept away on a wave that's purely *Adam*.

He pulls away, and I have to blink rapidly just to return to reality. Adam puts his arm around my shoulder and steers me through the crowd. "Arch!" Adam calls out as we turn into Actors' Alley.

A frown creases Arch's handsome face as he swiftly crosses to us. "What's up?" He glances from me to Adam.

"We have a problem," Adam says. "Joel tried to rape Melanie after dance auditions two nights ago."

Arch tips my face to the side and studies the road rash. When he's done, he glances back at Adam, his expression filled with reckless anger.

Adam tightens his hand on my good shoulder and nods. "I'm going to deal with Joel now, but you need to know there's a problem. The Drones will be gunning for Melanie after this."

"This has to stop," Arch says with a sneer. "He's been doing this kind of shit for a year, and no one's done anything about it."

We turn and head down the main walkway toward Quad One, where I spot Victoria's hallway guy.

To my surprise, Adam calls out to him. "Trey! Come here a sec."

The handsome boy smirks curiously as he approaches. "Adam, Arch." He gives a nod to each guy. "Judging from the looks on your faces, we're about to have some fun."

"Do you know Melanie?" Adam asks.

"Not formally, but I've noticed her."

"Haven't we all?" Adam says, amused.

Trey gives me a good-natured side-eye. "What's up?"

"Joel assaulted Melanie night before last," Adam explains. "Tried to rape her after the dance show auditions. I'm headed to deal with him and could use your help. Will you keep an eye on her?"

"I kind of already do." Trey's eyes narrow on me. "You okay?"

I nod shyly.

"I take it you two are together?" Trey asks.

Adam nods. "Not formally, but yes."

"I should've moved quicker," Trey returns with a sigh.

My eyes widen in surprise, and Adam throws back his head and belts a laugh.

"You're surprised?" he asks. "You seriously haven't figured out that basically all the guys at this school are chasing after you?"

I shrug and try not to blush.

"She's adorable," Trey says to Adam. Then, mercifully, he shifts topics. "You know I hate Joel. So what's the plan?"

Something seems to dawn on Adam. "How's your sister?"

"Thank God Arch walked in when he did." Trey turns to Arch. "Thank you, by the way. I owe you."

Arch shrugs it off.

"Kelsey's a freshman this year," Trey explains, looking to me. "It's been rough. The Drones terrorize her daily."

"I'll get my group to keep an eye on her," Arch says.

I'm growing frustrated and chime in. "For the record, I can handle Joel myself. I'm not particularly comfortable having all of you take care of this for me."

"Mel," Arch says, "you're part of my group now, and we're a family. I'm fully aware you can handle yourself, but we're not letting you do this alone."

"Hell no," Trey admonishes. "You're tiny. You aren't fighting Joel."

Adam snickers.

"Don't let her appearance fool you," Arch says. "Mel's a beast."

Before I can speak up on my own behalf, Adam gestures to the opposite end of the quad.

Joel. The sight of him makes my heart pound explosively. The trauma of what he did to me reverberates like an earthquake from my head to my toes, leaving me short of breath.

"Stay here," Adam says.

Arch and Trey turn, stalking after Adam into the impending fight.

I follow them, arriving in time to hear Joel snarl, "I'll do what I want."

"If you so much as *look* at any girl in this school again," Adam says, stepping closer to Joel, "I'll happily land my seething ass in jail."

Joel glowers at Adam, a slow, malicious smile spreading across his face.

My body quakes with the desire to run. When Joel's gaze shifts my way, his lips part suggestively, emitting a brutally sexual wave that makes my skin crawl.

This guy literally gets off on other people's fear.

I glance at Trey, and it's obvious from his expression that he feels it too. He reaches for my arm and pulls me behind him, shifting his body to block Joel's view.

"What do you two do?" Joel says with a nasty smirk. "Share her every other day?"

Adam looks to us for an instant, then, without answering, he strikes Joel with a punch to the gut. Joel doubles over.

Arch and Trey jump into the fight as nearby Drones lunge Adam's way. A full-scale brawl ensues as curious students gather around.

As things escalate, Tanner, Marcus, Hiram, and Kenji push through the crowd and rush into the fight, evening the odds.

Fists fly for only a few more seconds before a loud bellow freezes the bedlam.

Principal Walker wades through the crowd. "All of you, *stop*!" He levels the guys with a no-nonsense glare. "Who wants to explain this?"

"Joel tried to rape Melanie on campus after dance auditions,"

Adam says, gesturing to me. "In case you hadn't noticed, rape has become a nasty habit of his."

Principal Walker, clearly stunned and looking to confirm the charges, crosses to me and examines my injured face. When I lift my shirt, revealing the large black-and-purple bruise on my stomach, his brow creases.

"Joel," he says, pivoting, "do you have an explanation?"

Joel, shrugging, gives the principal an innocent look. "It wasn't me, I swear."

The principal turns back to me. "He said it wasn't him."

Now I'm pissed. I step up to Principal Walker and point Joel's way. "What about *his* face?"

Principal Walker moves in closer to Joel, looks him over, and lets out a sigh. "This does look questionable, Joel." He adds, "I'll be talking with your dad tomorrow. We're scheduled to meet for golf."

My eyebrows shoot into my hairline. *The principal is friends with Joel's dad?*

"This is bullshit!" Trey snarls.

"Trey Valdez!" Walker barks. "To the office! I won't be spoken to that way."

Trey scoffs. I watch him as he crosses the quad to grab his backpack, slinging it over his shoulder. He wheels around and shoots Principal Walker a death glare.

"Arch and Adam," the principal says, "I need you two to head to the office also."

Shock stiffens my spine. I prowl forward, stepping uncomfortably close to Principal Walker, and glare up at him. "You've got to be kidding?" I gesture to my friends. "*We're* the problem?"

Uncertainty flashes across his face.

"Joel tried to rape me! Either *you* deal with this, or *I* will."
Ferocity blasts from me in waves so strong they cause Adam's arms
to goosebump.

The principal has no answer.

"Good." I turn an icy glare on Joel. "My way's better."

Somewhere in the back of my mind, the disbelief that I've
allowed this side of me to take over registers. I've always known
it was there, but it had been buried deep under so many years of
insecurity I had almost forgotten it existed.

"You also," Walker says to me. "And you." He points to Joel.
"Let's go." He fires a thumb over his shoulder in the direction of
the two-story administration building.

My friends and I exchange silent glances.

"Not a chance in hell," I tell Principal Walker.

I turn and stalk off with the guys at my heels, headed off
campus through the alley.

When we get to the student parking lot, we turn to face each
other. I close my eyes and flex my back, internally evaluating the
"me" that has settled into my psyche. A slight smile graces my
lips when I realize I'm finally the Melanie I've always wanted
to be.

Adam grins down at me. "You good?"

"Hell, yes."

The guys laugh.

"You wanna have some fun?" Adam asks.

I nod, and he doesn't waste any time firing up the Harley.

⸺

"I have some people I want you to meet," Adam says. "One of
them's named Bear. This is his house. He'll be ditching school,

along with my other best friend Darren. Dante Grunier's band, Diablo, has a big gig tonight, and we'd planned to meet up today while they rehearse in the garage."

My eyebrows rise. *A ditch day to hang out with a band in a garage? Sounds pretty damn good.*

"You'll like them," Adam says. "But first, a warning: They're a little different."

He steers me through the open garage door, where a group of guys are standing around with their instruments. They fire up, and the noise is eardrum shattering. Adam guides me into the house and upstairs. When we enter one of the bedrooms, it's like being transported into another world full of lit candles and quiet.

Two boys sit facing each other in the middle of the room. Between them rests a stack of beautifully illustrated cards, with three of the cards placed face up. Intense concentration shows on the face of both boys. Adam gives me an encouraging smile. Apparently, we're safe in this mysterious sanctuary.

I find myself standing and watching the unfamiliar game as Adam sits on the bed, lounging with a pillow propped behind his back. He motions for me to join him. I climb onto the bed, awkward in my skirt, and lean against his side. I'm nervous at first about how this could be a ploy to get me into an amorous situation, but he's totally relaxed as we sit and watch the duo.

The two guys stretch their backs. From the way they move, it's clear they've been sitting in the same position for a long time, focusing on whatever game they're playing. The nearest of the two stands, and at once the room feels smaller. He's a mountain of a boy. Even his energy is huge. He cocks his head back at Adam, wondering who I am.

"This is my best friend Bear," Adam tells me. "Bear, this is Melanie."

Before I can respond, Bear belts the biggest, most exuberant laugh I've ever heard. The sound booms and echoes, bouncing off the walls. When it finally dies out, I feel rejuvenated somehow.

"Well, hello, Kitten Little. Aren't you a sight for sore eyes!" Bear observes me with curiosity. "What's your sign?"

Taken by surprise, I laugh and answer, "Aries. Why?"

Bear and Darren side-eye each other before hitting Adam with twin amusement.

"Damn, Adam," Darren says. "You're going to have your hands full with this one. She's a cardinal fire sign."

Adam smirks and nods subtly. "Yeah. I've figured that out already."

I grin slightly and hit him with an over-the-top innocent expression, chirping, "I don't have any idea what you're talking about."

Adam tips his head back, belting surprised laughter.

"I like this one," Bear says to Adam. "She's got good energy. Don't hurt her, or I'll have to hurt you."

He pounces playfully on Adam, and I wiggle and roll, barely making it out of the way of Bear's massive attack before coming face-to-face with the other guy—*Darren, was it?*—who has long black braids, a dark complexion, and is wearing a black T-shirt and well-worn jeans. He's beautiful in an ethereal, old-soul sort of way. Like he's been transported from another time, or he's on his hundredth lifetime. I'm perched on the edge of the bed, one leg on the floor and one leg under me, frozen halfway through the motion of fleeing the Adam-and-Bear scrum. I must look ridiculous.

"Madam, your name again?" he asks.

I finish climbing off the bed and manage not to stumble. When Darren looks down into my eyes, it's as though he's staring into my soul, exposing my secrets.

"Melanie," I answer, and since I've become a version of myself who always speaks her mind, I add, "Your energy's so smooth, and kind of ancient. I'm sorry. I'm feeling a little disoriented. I must sound like an idiot."

Darren's smile lights his face. "Actually, a surprisingly accurate description. Rather intuitive of you, Melanie. I do believe you may be one of us."

"What game are you playing?" I ask.

Darren looks down at the cards. "It's not a game, actually. It's a tarot deck I designed." I must look confused because he follows with, "Tarot decks are like fortune-teller cards. You ask a question, and then someone who knows how to read the cards—me, for instance—can give you an answer."

Now this *is fascinating*. I've never heard of tarot, but I'm suddenly alive with curiosity. "The cards are beautiful. You made them yourself?"

He smiles proudly, then turns to the other two, who are winded from their childish wrestling match. "Melanie's new to tarot. But she can't be that new to our world because she's wearing a wicked clear quartz pendant."

Bear's eyes widen and Adam nods. "I got it for her."

Darren turns back to me and gestures to my necklace. "May I?"

When I nod, he gently puts his hand under the stone, studying it carefully.

"It's beautiful," he says after a time. Gently, he lets it settle back on my chest.

"Well!" Bear says as he gracefully sinks to the floor. No boy the size of a mountain should be able to move as effortlessly as that. "We should have Kitten Little ask a question."

I look to Adam, who gives a nod. "I'm going to go listen to a song that Dante needs chord help with. You're safe with these guys, Melanie. I trust them." He squeezes my hand and heads out the door.

Darren and Bear gesture to a spot for me on the floor beside the cards.

Why not? Let's give this tarot stuff a shot.

If nothing else, the quiet, warm energy of this room is intoxicatingly cozy. I step forward and lower myself carefully. Wearing a skirt doesn't lend itself well to sitting cross-legged on the floor with two strangers, but they're both so consumed with shuffling the tarot deck they barely seem to notice I'm here. I close my eyes and inhale, realizing that Bear's cologne smells like palo santo and dragon's blood. Something about it warms me all the way through.

I can't quite put my finger on why these guys aren't your normal teenagers, but then it hits me. Their focus is on a level that most teenagers could never rise to. They don't seem to need constant motion, always doing and talking. These two are Zen.

"All right, Melanie," Bear says. "First, you ask a question, hand on the deck."

I only have to think for a second before the question comes to me. "Am I meant to date Adam?"

Both guys chuckle, low and deep.

Darren looks across at Bear. "I already know the answer to that, but we can give the cards a chance. *You* need to read the cards for her on this one."

Bear nods.

"Now pick just one card," Darren instructs me. He fans the cards out with practiced hands. "This question only needs a one-card answer."

I close my eyes and hover my hand over the cards, not sure what I'm doing. Instinct tells me to move my hand slowly and wait until I can sense which one to take. *There!* I slide out the card and hand it to Darren.

"What were you doing just now when you picked that card?" Bear's tone is almost shockingly nonjudgmental.

"I guess I went with instinct," I offer. "Something told me to run my hand over the cards with my eyes closed and wait until I felt a change. That card was a little warmer than the rest, so I picked it."

"Excellent job, Kitten Little. She's definitely one of us," he says to Darren.

Darren nods, and a genuine smile flashes briefly on his serious face. He passes the card to his friend.

"All right," Bear says grandly. "Moment of truth. Let's see what you picked." He studies the card. "Hm. The three of hearts." His expression shifts to disappointment. "That's a no-go, Kitten Little. I'm sorry. Though, we could have told you that. He's a great guy, and we love him, but Adam needs a girl who'll throw caution to the wind and make daring choices with him. Someone like Valerie, perhaps. You, much like Presley and Finley before you, aren't prepared to meet Adam where he lives. You, in particular, have a deep intuition that won't allow you to dive into his energetic chaos, at least not yet." Bear's eyes are soft, as if he's hoping he hasn't hurt me.

Sigh. Well, there goes that. I glance down, disappointed. "I really thought there was something between us."

Both guys laugh and shake their heads.

"Honestly," Darren says, "every girl Adam has brought around has thought the same thing."

"There's good news, though," Bear says. "That guy will always have your back. He's a loyal friend, and that'll last long after you two are done with this little game you're playing. Stay friends. It's worth having Adam on your side."

"He taught me how to channel and ground my energy," I say, still grappling with the unfortunate revelation. "Seemed like there was something more there than the usual player bullshit."

Bear and Darren exchange a look.

"Interesting," Bear says.

"How did the card tell you all that, by the way?" I ask.

"The three of hearts indicates a mismatched pair that won't work no matter how hard you try. What's interesting is the number three, though. It suggests there's a third person—someone close by who'll come into the picture. That one's the guy. Keep an eye out for him. You'll know."

Before I can respond to this mind-blowing tidbit, the door opens, and Adam slips back into the room.

CHAPTER *16*

I lean my head back and stare up at the stars above the open courtyard. *Unbelievable.*

I check my pager again—twenty-three minutes late and counting. An unexpected nervousness creeps through me. After a day of shopping, I had Finley drop me off at Mann's Chinese Theater on Hollywood Boulevard. I'm supposed to meet Adam for a movie, but it appears he has stood me up. I had no intention of being alone in Hollywood on a Saturday night. Yet, here I am.

I'm beyond irritated. *Looks like he's just as bad as they said.*

I decide to call Mom to come pick me up. I head through the courtyard, stepping over the footprints of superstars of the Golden Age of Cinema that grace the sidewalk. Tourists laugh as they compare their own hands to the cement prints, forever frozen in time.

There's an oddness to Hollywood Boulevard, especially after dark. I'm keenly aware of the combination of glamour and grunge, especially apparent tonight as I turn the corner and head to a pay phone a block away.

I'm halfway there when suddenly ahead I spot Joel and three of his Drones walking toward me coming from the opposite direction. Joel smiles sadistically when his eyes catch mine. They're all wearing their usual black-and-white dresswear, their posh appearance out of sync with the malicious vibe they're radiating.

"Target in sight," Stan says. He's the only one of Joel's posse that I recognize, and he's bad news.

My heart starts pounding in my throat. I turn and run, knowing there's no time to hesitate. A quick left, and I bolt through a tourist gift shop full of plastic Academy Award gag gifts and tacky trinkets. Things crash behind me as the Drones bulldoze their way through the store, their feet pounding close behind me. I gasp as I barrel toward the back of the building.

Where do I go? There!

I skid right at the back of the store and bolt through a door labeled *Restrooms*. It dumps me into a long, poorly lit hallway. It's not what I expected, but there has to be somewhere to hide. I try the first door on the right, but it's locked. The door to the hall behind me slams against the wall as the Drones pour in.

I try the next door. It opens and I rush through, surprised to find myself in the neighboring store. The blasting of White Zombie's "Black Sunshine" fuels my feet as I race through the vintage clothing boutique. I get to the counter near the front and turn just in time to see Joel rounding the edge of a rack full of leather pants and band Ts. Waves of rage and battle lust roll off him.

He stops, meeting my wide-eyed gaze, and grins. *He's loving this.*

My eyes dart right, then left. The Drones have me surrounded.

The tough-looking shop owner figures out I'm in trouble and makes a grab for Joel. When the Drones turn on the guy, I use the distraction to my advantage and bolt through the front door.

I skid left and take off at a sprint, my feet pounding down the star-paved sidewalk. Seeing a girl running for her life isn't all that uncommon in this city where people typically mind their own business. People turn and stare, but no one helps. *Maybe some cornfed midwestern tourist who doesn't know the local custom of not giving a shit will help me.* The thought almost makes me laugh, but it's washed away on a fresh wave of terror as I hear feet striking the pavement behind me.

"Get her!" Joel yells.

I can't keep this up! He's right behind me! My lungs are screaming, having gone well beyond my second wind. Just when I think there's no way I can take another step, a seventies-era black sports car rumbles through the intersection and pulls into a parking spot near the end of the block. The engine stops and the driver-side door opens. Trey jumps out, slams the door, and runs around the front of his car to the sidewalk.

Thank God!

I dart behind him and skid to a stop. Panting and exhausted, I lean against the hood of his car. Between all the fear and adrenaline, I briefly see stars.

Trey rushes at Joel, who catches him with a right hook to the eye. It doesn't slow Trey down. Within seconds, Trey has Joel flat on his back on the pavement. Apparently, Trey's reputation as a bruiser precedes him because the other three Drones back away. They turn and take off down the sidewalk, leaving Joel to fend for himself.

Trey reaches down and grabs the front of Joel's shirt, heaving him up with one arm. He yanks Joel in close and snarls, "If you *ever* touch Melanie or my sister again, I swear to *God* it'll be the last thing you do!" He draws back his fist and coldcocks Joel, whose head lolls to the side. Trey lets go, dropping him.

Trey turns to me, his eyes clouded with battle-rage.

My mouth flops open. *Hot!* The thought makes me laugh. *Why do I always do that? Every time danger has passed, I have a moment of temporary hysteria.*

Trey stalks to me. "What's so funny?"

I look down and grin before meeting his eyes. "Honestly, I was just thinking that you're hot. It amused me, given the life-and-death situation I just went through."

Clearly, I've taken him by surprise because he barks a laugh. "You're an odd one."

"You're mad at me," I say. "Explain."

He scowls. "What the *hell* are you doing on Hollywood Boulevard, *alone and at night*?"

I don't bother hiding my annoyance. "I wasn't supposed to be alone. Adam asked me to meet him for a movie at Mann's, but he stood me up."

Trey looks surprised before his expression shifts to irritation. Finally, he lands on what looks like hopeful consideration. He narrows his eyes a touch and gives me a slight, sly smile.

"What are you thinking?" I ask.

"I'm thinking I owe Adam a giant thank-you. Hell, I might even buy him a bouquet of flowers."

"Why's that?"

"Because I wanted a shot with you, and he just stepped out of the way."

I shake my head and laugh, surprised.

Trey's expression softens. "Are you okay?"

"At this point, I don't even know anymore." I look up at him. "If you're asking if I'm physically hurt, then no. I'm not. At least not any more than I was at the start of the day." I smile slightly. "Thank you, Trey. Your timing was charmed."

I reach out, touching face. His left eye is already starting to swell.

"I'm sorry about your eye."

"It was worth it," he says with a hint of flirtation. "I happen to have the evening free. You up for salvaging your date night?"

I grin and glance down, considering the option. *He's gorgeous, and I've been intrigued for a while. Why not?* I look up at him and nod.

He smiles and says, "There's a laser show set to Pink Floyd's 'Dark Side of the Moon' at the Griffith Park Observatory." He clicks on his pager, checking the time. "Starts in forty-five minutes. Any chance you're into psychedelic rock?"

Perfect! "You have no idea how good that sounds," I say. "I actually suggested it to Adam, but he wasn't into it."

Trey grins. "I would love to take you." He gestures toward his car, and I step over to the passenger side. He unlocks the door for me.

"What kind of car is this?" I ask as I slide into the passenger seat.

"It's a '79 Camaro Z28. I've been fixing it up. It still needs work, but I love it."

The cabin smells like exhaust, warm leather, and Trey's cologne. *CK One . . . nice.*

Trey rounds the front of the car, gets in, and puts the key in the ignition. The car rumbles to life, and the engine sounds like an evil creature. I'm into it.

Trey smiles at me, and we take off.

CHAPTER *17*

A wave of nostalgia washes over me as we enter the Griffith Park Observatory. I haven't been here since a field trip in the third grade. They usually show educational films about constellations and astronomy. I can't wait to find out how different tonight will be.

It's not too crowded. Trey turns into the back row, stops in the middle, and sits down. I sit beside him and look up. The seats tip back a bit, and I rest my head on the headrest, taking in the massive dome above.

When the lights dim, I exhale, content.

The gentle sound of "Speak to Me / Breathe" trickles through the air as beams of light begin to appear. My eyes widen in awe at the acoustic perfection of this building. With its intoxicating combination of light and dark, the album is one of my favorites, and it's coming through on a level I've never heard before. Faint screaming wafts through the song as the show opens into a melodic world. Much like a dance, the laser beams paint the music. I drift away, mesmerized.

I exhale deeply and my shoulders go slack. I feel Trey's eyes on me and turn to find him staring with a soft expression. There's something new in his eyes.

Something starts to unwrap in my mind—like a dormancy that suddenly awakens. My eyes widen a touch and I stare into space. I wait, watching internally, as it unfolds in layers I can't control.

A new layer reveals itself, and intuitive awareness blows gently through my chest, radiating lightly down my spine. *Something about my life is changing*, I realize. *Right here, right now.*

The thought is swept away as the song bleeds into "On the Run." The hypnotic ticking and faint subconscious voices pick up in the music, followed by the sound of running feet and heavy breathing. My heart rate picks up and my lips part. The lasers create the image of a person running, being chased by vague, evil images. It stirs up the memory of Joel's attack, and with it comes a wave of fear. Tears fill my eyes as I hold out my hands and survey the unexpected trembling.

Trey leans over and whispers, "I didn't realize how close to home some of this would be. We can leave if you need to get out of here."

Without looking his way, I shake my head, and whisper back, "I don't want to give you the impression that I'm insane, but a lot's happening in my head right now. I need to work through whatever this is."

"Interesting," he breathes as he settles back in his chair.

His gaze stays on me as the experience continues. I wait as every emotion I can imagine riffles through me on a wave of energy I don't understand.

The music booms, and after the silence stretches, it shifts to "Time." Clocks and alarms loudly chime and ring. My mind screams, *This is the time you've been waiting for! Ghost Melanie is officially gone! You've stepped into your own!* The realization sends me reeling. My breath comes in ragged gasps. I close my eyes and look inward, watching as my energy shifts and slowly remolds in my psyche. My mind zeroes in on the repetitive tick-tock beat running in the background.

"Melanie?" Trey whispers.

I don't answer. *I have to get through this metamorphosis.* I know it seems crazy, but what I'm experiencing is at once beautiful in its simplicity and overwhelmingly complicated. I wait, open, for the next layer to unfold. I hold my breath and look back up at the dome. The laser show streams and drifts in what seems like a thousand colors all blending and swirling, painting the picture of the energy in my head. I'm lost in the show again, and my muscles relax one at a time. I inhale, gather the slightly erratic energy, and exhale it down and out.

Trey catches my attention with a sharp sound that escapes his lips. He's staring at me with wide eyes.

"You okay?" I murmur.

He nods slightly. "I've got a lot happening in my head."

I smile and return to watching the show. *Looks like I'm not the only one having a metamorphosis.* My intuition connects to the thought and nags at me a bit, but I push it gently aside as the piano introduction to "The Great Gig in the Sky" begins. This is my favorite Pink Floyd song. The lasers gently wave, creating something like a borealis effect. My heart rate drops, and I settle again into the moment, drifting from reality. Trey takes my hand as the captivating voice of the female vocalist rings out over the music.

Suddenly, every muscle in my body tenses as a raging storm of unchecked energy builds both painfully slow and so fast that my mind sputters. It's overwhelming, nearly to the point of tearing me apart.

Time stops.

I gasp and my mouth falls open.

I see stars.

The energy explodes from me, straight through my hand and into Trey.

He tenses and whispers, "Oh . . . my . . . God."

My gaze shifts and he turns to me.

I look down at our hands as the energy courses between us, melding and weaving with a heart-stopping synergy.

How can something this powerful be invisible?

His expression is a mix of shock and wonder that nearly stops my pounding heart.

"You felt that?" I whisper.

Wide-eyed, he nods. "I need to talk to you. Now."

We stand and he pulls me up the dark aisle and out the planetarium doors, leaving the cash register ka-chings of "Money" in our wake. He leads me briskly through the towering, ornately golden lobby and through the massive front doors of the observatory. As the fresh night air hits us, Trey drops my hand and leans over, hands on his knees, as he tries to catch his breath. I close my eyes and attempt to wrap my mind around what just happened.

When I open my eyes, Trey's standing upright again, staring at me. He turns and walks across the expanse to the west observation deck. I follow, and together we stop and take in the view of Hollywood below.

"How much energy work have you done?" Trey asks.

"Literally the only thing I know is what Adam taught me a few days ago. Grounding and centering."

He nods absently. "Then I'm a lot further ahead of you on that journey."

"You do energy work? I thought it was rare."

"It is. But you've got an irresistible energy, so you're going to attract guys who feel it." He smiles ruefully. "Adam and I are two of those guys. Unfortunately, so is Joel."

I ponder for a moment and decide to trust Trey. "I've had an uncanny sense of intuition since I was little. I know things are going to happen before they do, but I have no control over it. Adam suspects it's connected to an undeveloped psychic gift. A lot has been happening lately. Things are shifting."

He chuckles almost to himself. "I hate to tell you, but it's about to become more complicated."

I tilt my head. "Yeah? Explain."

His nervousness shows as he swallows deeply and stares out at the view, gathering his thoughts. After what feels like an eternity, he turns back to me. "Ground out first. I need you calm for this."

I close my eyes and focus inward, drawing my nervous energy together and grounding it down and out. When I open my eyes, he's smiling.

"You just learned to do that?"

I nod.

"You're going to be a force to reckon with when you get control of all of this." He holds out his hand and hits me with a serious look.

I hesitantly put my hand in his. Again our energy wraps and melds as it did during the show, but it's less overwhelming this time. I close my eyes to examine the process. A sudden pulse of what feels like love thrums through my hand.

My eyes snap open.

"I've always wondered who you would be," Trey says, smiling softly. "And if I'd find you. A lot of people never do. I promised myself that I'd be open and aware enough to realize it when you arrived, but I didn't expect it to be so overwhelmingly obvious."

Confused, I furrow my brow. "You just met me, Trey. What are you talking about?"

He shakes his head. "I didn't just meet you. We've known each other." He squeezes my hand, and the energy swells. He shifts my hand around to lace his fingers with mine. Then he does the same with my other hand. The energy suddenly meets on both sides, creating a circle that hums with a calm perfection unlike anything I've ever experienced. My eyes close and my head lolls forward. My breathing is even. My heart rate slows. Everything in my body hums, synchronized on a level I've never known before.

I feel at home in my own skin.

When he lets go of my left hand, the perfect synergy lightens, but it's still there. I open my eyes, disappointed to lose the intensity of a feeling I fear I'll never experience again.

Trey tips up my chin and kisses me. Fire races up my back, and my chest rises as my intuition swells nearly to bursting. My fingers tingle, the sensation spreading from our clasped hands through my body. Our lips still pressed together, I gasp and my knees give out. Trey snakes an arm around my waist and lifts me off the ground. As the kiss slows, my heart rate picks up. We're left unmoving, consumed in the moment, our lips pressed together.

Finally, he pulls away and sets me down.

I feel like I've been lost and found all at the same time. I rest my forehead on his chest, trying to put the pieces of myself back together. Trey wraps his arms around me, his hands shaky against my back. The scent of his cologne sucks the tension out of my body. I sag against him as he exhales.

He feels and smells like home. Weird that it's a home I don't know at all. But somehow, I know everything about him.

After a long moment, he says, "It's called a soulmate connection, Melanie, and we've got it."

CHAPTER 18

Arch's headlights flash across the observatory parking lot as he pulls into a spot. He's quickly followed by Kenji, Finley, and Bear in each of their cars. The last to rumble through the lot is Adam, with Valerie on the back of his Harley.

I roll my eyes. *Well, now I know why he didn't show up.*

Trey leans in and asks, "You good?"

I nod.

My friends pour out of the cars and gather around us. *Looks like Trey's phone call to Arch was taken seriously.* Trey's leaning on the stone railing with his arm draped around my shoulders.

My gaze cuts to Adam. "Can I speak with you?"

Adam nods, and Trey lets me go.

Adam and I cross to the opposite side of the lot, where I stop and turn to him. I raise my eyebrows expectantly, but he does nothing more than look confused.

I roll my eyes. "Date? Tonight? You and me? You stood me up?"

Awareness floods his expression. "Shit. I'm so sorry, Melanie. I got sidetracked."

"Sidetracked? Is that what we're calling Valerie now? She'll *love* that."

He grimaces. After a long pause, he offers, "I'll have Arch take Valerie home and make tonight up to you."

A sarcastic chuckle bubbles up and escapes my mouth. "You're a completely vibrant shithead. You're intoxicating, but you've got a lot to learn about the effects of toying with people."

I turn on my heel and walk off before he has a chance to respond. When I rejoin the group, I squeeze past Bear and Darren on my way to Trey. The two side-eye each other, sensing that I'm irritable.

Trey reaches out a hand to me, and the moment we touch, the irritation is replaced with a wave of contentment. *God help me. I need time to work through this with him. I've never felt this safe, and yet somehow I find it terrifying.*

As if to answer my thought, Trey murmurs, "We'll talk about it, but I promise you're okay. I'm not going anywhere."

Softly, so no one else can hear, I whisper, "How did you know—"

He places a finger to my lips and then drops his hand, lacing his fingers through mine. A pulse rolls through his hands and into me. It's almost like an energy-emotion bubble. It's not really a thought in words, more like a three-dimensional feeling. My eyes widen a touch when I realize the bubble carries layers of me being *his*. I meet his gaze, and his lips curl with the slightest smile.

One of the guys clears his throat. When I look up, Bear is grinning at me.

"That didn't take long," he says with a wink. "I see you found the guy we talked about."

When I grin, he gives a knowing nod.

"Why don't you two fill us in on why we're here?" Bear says. "Then we can leave you to your exciting soulmate connection."

Adam looks questioningly at Bear, who shrugs. Adam is clearly agitated, and he shoots Trey a nasty glare. Trey meets it, unflinching, as he pulls me against him with my back to his chest. I exhale and rest my head against his shoulder.

"Melanie," Trey says, "do you want to fill them in?"

Let Trey deal with this. He can handle it. "Nope," I say. "I just want to *be*."

He chuckles and then kisses me behind the ear, sending tingles up my spine.

"All right," Trey says. "Here it is. Most of you know by now that Melanie was attacked after the dance auditions."

Everyone nods.

"So, imagine my surprise when I'm stopped at the light at Hollywood and Highland earlier tonight, and I spot Melanie hauling ass down the sidewalk with Joel and three of his Drones quick on her tail."

I feel Trey's energy shift and can sense he's hitting Adam with a pointed look because Adam suddenly appears wracked with guilt.

"I pulled over and confronted the four," Trey continues, "and I got this black eye out of the deal. I demanded to know why the *hell* Melanie was alone on Hollywood Boulevard at night, and she informed me that Adam stood her up for a date to the movies."

A couple of the guys groan, and all eyes shift to Adam.

Valerie glares up at him. "You were supposed to be on a date with Melanie tonight?"

When he nods, she crosses her arms and looks down.

"I'm so sorry, Melanie," she says. "I had no idea."

Rather than reply, I shift my gaze to Adam, who's now glancing between Val and me.

Valerie sighs. "Adam, Melanie's my friend. I didn't realize you two had a thing, or tonight never would've happened." She turns my way and starts to apologize again, but I wave her off.

"I'm good," I say. "Whatever. Have fun."

Adam appears insulted by my casual dismissal of him. Everyone looks confused by my blasé response, but it's quickly cleared up when I lace my fingers through Trey's. I close my eyes and relax my back against his chest again, letting my head droop contentedly to the side.

Trey laughs, the sound vibrating through my back.

"Clearly, we've missed some things," Marcus says. "Melanie's usually pensive and now she looks like a cat who found a sunspot for a nap."

"Yeah, you missed some things." Trey squeezes my hands. "Anyhow, with Melanie's evening suddenly becoming free, I asked her on a date to the laser show. We realized we've got a connection."

"A *connection*?" Presley chirps. "I want one of those connections. Melanie looks high."

Everyone cracks up.

"I assume," Arch chimes in, "that we're not here to witness the beginnings of you two falling madly in love."

"Don't worry," Trey says. "I'll get to the point. I'm dying to get you all the hell out of here so Mel and I can be alone."

I laugh and glance at Bear, who winks.

"Once upon a recent time, my sister was nearly raped by Joel," Trey says, "who has now attacked Melanie *twice*."

"Joel tried to rape me at a party last year," Valerie says. "Adam walked in and stopped things before they escalated, but I know what that psychopath was planning to do. That guy has the evilest vibes I've ever felt."

Her description is so accurate that I shudder. I feel tears well as it sinks in just how close I came to getting truly hurt. Trey loosens his arms around me, and I turn to face him. He pulls me in, his arms resting on my back, keeping me safe. I close my eyes and press my head to his chest.

"Joel is dangerous," Trey says. "This we know. The three Drones with him tonight were just as enthusiastic about chasing Melanie. We're clearly not going to get any support from the school administration. It's time we dealt with this ourselves."

We all exchange sly smiles, and the mood shifts with mounting danger and anticipation. It's no secret this group loves a good rumble.

Arch cracks his knuckles. "I'm game."

Adam nods, glancing between me and Valerie, who have both been on the receiving end of Joel's assaults. He crosses the brief distance and turns my face away from Trey's chest, examining my still-healing road rash.

Trey grips the side of my face and radiates challenge as he glares at Adam. He pulls my head back to rest on his chest.

Adam sighs and crosses back to Valerie. From the corner of my eye, I can see he's still watching me, and I sense his regret about brushing me aside for her.

Trey's competitive vibe fuels my conviction, and the part of me I usually keep under lock and key roils from my depths. I look up to him and proclaim loudly enough for the entire group to hear, "Joel's mine to deal with. Monday, first thing."

Trey, clearly confused, says, "Not a chance, Melanie. I'm dealing with him."

My grin laced with danger, I step away.

I turn to Arch and raise an eyebrow questioningly. Arch leads the group, and if he agrees with me, I'll have the leverage I need.

Arch levels Trey with a speculative look, and after a moment's pause, he says, "She's tougher than she looks. If we're all there to back her, I vote we give her a shot."

Bear nods. "Joel won't hit a girl in front of a crowd at school."

Adam looks at Bear like he's insane and growls, "He gut-kicked her! Joel doesn't give a shit that she's a girl."

I snap my head Adam's way. "Then it's a good thing I don't give a shit that I'm a girl, either. I'm dealing with him, with or without the group's help." I survey my friends, challenge brimming in my eyes. "Your choice."

Presley grins. "Hell yeah! I'll back you. We'll get suspended! I could use a week off."

Arch shakes his head. "The goal needs to be to get Principal Walker to understand that he's let this go too far. Joel and the Drones need to be expelled."

"I've been thinking about Joel's patterns," Finley interjects quietly. "And I worry Melanie is only going to rev him up."

"Explain," Arch says.

I lean my back against Trey as Finley gathers her thoughts.

He whispers into my ear, "We need to discuss this."

I shake my head, while staring up at the stars. "I'm a brass-balls bitch, Trey. You don't know me yet. Hell, I'm still figuring me out, but I'm telling you I've got this."

Adam, clearly intrigued, turns his attention to me and gives a flirtatious wink. I roll my eyes and gesture subtly with a slight tip of the head to Valerie.

His fumes quietly at my dismissal.

"My mom's a therapist," Finley says. "I've learned a few things about people like Joel. We already know his brain isn't wired right, but I think it's worse than we know." She glances my way. "He's attacked Melanie twice. Think about it. What's he after?"

Everyone stares at me blankly.

"Murder?" Tanner replies.

Finley shakes her head. "The exact opposite." She gestures to Valerie. "Kelsey and Val were attacked, unprovoked, early on, and facing the threat of Arch and Adam was enough to stop Joel. But"—her gaze shifts back to me—"Mr. Mental Illness was just starting to get his freak on back then. He's had time and, I'm guessing, plenty of opportunity to perfect his game. I'm sure there are girls we don't know about. Mental illness is a progressive process, and I've seen the way he watches Melanie. Joel's obsessed."

She hits me with the weight of her serious stare. "He's always lurking in the shadows watching you, Melanie. And when he thinks no one is paying attention, he lets his inner freak shine through. Parting his lips, panting seductively." Her gaze shifts to Trey. "He's not going to stop until he has her."

"You think this is about Joel wanting to date Melanie?" Trey asks, his tone skeptical.

"No," Finley replies with a shake of the head. "I think this is about Joel *needing* to dominate her. He's that sick."

Trey, eyes wide, looks down at me. He puts a hand on the back of my head and pulls me to him, crushing me against his chest. "Does the level of screwed-up that Finley's describing track with what's already happened?"

"His hand was on my face while I was crying, and he sucked my tears off his fingers like he was eating barbeque. Before he kicked me in the gut and took off, he licked my face from my chin to my temple. He also told me that the terror in my eyes was what was gonna do it for him."

Trey goes still and I wiggle away. One glance at his face reveals his slack-jawed shock.

I don't give him time to argue with me and turn, nodding at Finley. "I'm going to kick his ass either way. If it fuels his obsession, then I'll kick his ass again." I look to Arch. "Make a plan that gets me in front of Joel first thing Monday morning. I'm taking my shot at him. Bent-ass little boys need to be taught a lesson."

"Maybe we can kill two birds with one stone," Arch says. "If we can rid ourselves of Joel, as well as the entire student council, the whole school will be a better place. The Drones are just as bad as he is. The school will never be safe as long as those assholes are in charge."

Everyone nods.

"What happens to homecoming if the student council is gone?" Marcus asks. "Not that they've done jack shit for planning so far. Still, I'm looking forward to the dance."

Arch answers, "No clue. That's Principal Walker's problem."

"All right," Trey says. "Let's all plan to meet on the front lawn at seven forty-five on Monday."

"Dress to impress. School colors," Arch orders. "I want everyone prepared to intimidate. If we're walking Melanie into a showdown, we're gonna do it with flair."

"I still haven't agreed to that," Trey says.

Adam scoffs. "Good luck with *that*." He tips his head my way. "Firecracker here is a force to be reckoned with. I wonder if you can handle her, Trey."

I look up at Trey, and he meets my gaze with smoldering intensity.

For Adam's benefit, I say, "I don't."

Trey smiles with an edge of amorous challenge and the rest of the group, tactfully, takes their leave.

CHAPTER *19*

It's seven-forty on Monday morning, and half of us have arrived at the designated meeting place in front of the school. I'm nervously standing here in my black miniskirt, red cropped sweater, and heels, as we wait for the rest of the group to arrive. My chestnut hair is curled dramatically, and I channeled my "inner Tanner," with my harsh eye makeup and blood-red lips. I'm into it. Might be my new thing.

Finley, Bear, Darren, Tanner, Kenji, and Presley, all looking posh and sleek, arrived just after me, and I spot Hiram and Arch walking toward us now from across the street. Arch flashes devil horns, and Darren and Tanner, smiling at the pair, return the greeting.

A Harley growls around the corner, and Adam appears, dressed all in black. Val, perched on the back of his bike, is wearing a flaming-red skintight minidress and red heels—a gutsy choice, given her ride today. I grin because it appears the two have really hit it off. I'm thoroughly over Adam. After Adam parks, Val somehow manages to slide off the back of the bike without flashing anyone. The couple greet us, looking so good it should be illegal.

Marcus pulls up across the street in his dad's Porsche and climbs out of the car.

I bite my lip, worried because I haven't heard from Trey since he dropped me off at home Saturday night. I laugh quietly to myself. According to my parents, he and I were quite entertaining during our explanation as to why Trey was dropping me off, rather than Adam.

They seem to like Trey, though.

I feel Trey's energy before I see him walking around the corner of the two-story building. He's dressed in a red muscle tank, black jeans, and wearing a pair of Oakley sunglasses.

"Yo, Mel," Arch says with a wink, "your boy's here." Arch turns to Trey and shouts, "Better late than never, loser!"

Trey grins.

I bounce down the stairs and run to greet him. He stops to brace himself as I leap into his arms. He scoops me up, my legs around his waist, and grins.

Good thing I'm wearing bicycle shorts under my skirt, or I would've just mooned everyone.

"I missed you," he says, looking deep into my eyes.

"I missed you too." I give him a stern look. "We need to work on this whole you not calling me after Saturday night issue."

He laughs. "Noted. I apologize. I was busy tying up some loose ends." He leans in, his lips almost touching mine. "I promise I'll make it up to you." When he kisses me, my stomach erupts with butterflies.

We're interrupted by our jackass friends, who call out in unison, "Ooooh!"

I glare up to the lawn and snark back, "I hate you guys!"

Trey sets me down as everyone laughs. He drapes an arm around my shoulder as we join the rest of the group.

"Everyone looks great," Arch says. "Now we need to march into that school like we own the place. Make sure everyone knows we aren't to be messed with. The plan is to find Joel and give Melanie a crack at him. Only if something goes awry, do we step in. Got it?"

Everyone nods.

"You ready for this, Melanie?" Bear asks.

"You bet your ass I am." I talk a good game, but inside I'm a nervous wreck. I grip my crystal, close my eyes, and center myself, grounding down and out my nervous energy. Now feeling prepared, I open my eyes and say confidently, "Let's do this."

Adam smiles at me, then throws a side-eye to Trey. "I see you're still wearing the pendant I gave you on our date."

"I am. Thank you again."

"That was a good day, right?"

Trey rolls his eyes, and Valerie throws Adam a look of disgust.

"Childish much?" she says.

Adam looks bewildered, oblivious, apparently, that he's hitting on me while his girlfriend is standing right beside him.

I decide it's best to ignore his question, and we all line up in pairs.

Val turns to Presley, Finley, and me. "Showtime, girls. Let's give everyone at this school a taste of what they're missing." She flashes her fiercest smile, but it fades quickly. "Melanie, I really am sorry."

I shake my head and smile softly. "You have *no* idea how much I've gained because Adam didn't show up. You and I are good."

Trey smiles at Val, who glances curiously between him and me. It's apparent she's stunned by our rapid love connection.

Arch and Hiram take point, both wearing no-nonsense expressions to go with their kick-ass trench coats. The rest of the guys look ready to take on the world. Arch throws up a double set of devil horns. The girls' heel-clad feet click aggressively as we strut across the lacquered floor. The hall, full of students, is uncharacteristically quiet. People whisper and gawk, some with their mouths hanging open. One by one, we're joined by nearly every kid we pass. Few are able to resist the dangerous Pied Piper vibe we're emitting.

As we exit the two-story building, I experience a brief intuition flash. "They're waiting at our usual table," I warn the others.

"Your intuition?" Bear asks.

"Uh-huh."

We round the corner into Actors' Alley, where Joel and the Drones are lying in wait and looking to bring trouble our way.

They want a fight? Fine! They've got one!

We drop our backpacks in a pile beside one of the bungalows and line up opposite the Drones, who are flanked by Victoria and her minions—all of whom are staring daggers at me.

Victoria slinks forward, her eyes laser focused on mine. She stops dead center between the rival groups, her stance aggressive. "Do you really think *you* are going to make *that* work?" She gestures to Trey standing beside me, his arm around my waist.

I roll my eyes. "You're a snotty bitch who needs to mind her own business."

"Don't do this, Tori," Trey says.

Tori?

"Seriously?" she counters. "That's not what you said a few weeks ago when we were parked on Mulholland Drive."

The crowd lets loose a collective, "Oooooh!"

My stomach drops, recalling the first day of school when Victoria was hitting on Trey.

Mouth agape, I whip my head to him. "You've got to be kidding me."

"Melanie doesn't know about us?" Victoria brings a sarcastically innocent hand to her mouth, then drops it to her side. "How do you like my sloppy seconds?"

I meet her icy gaze, and then turn back to Trey. "Gross, Trey!" His face has gone slack.

Victoria, distracting him from my steely gaze, steps forward and stares at me as she runs a hand across Trey's chest. "It was good to see you yesterday, Trey."

The crowd lets loose another childish, "Oooooh!"

After her parting shot, Victoria turns on her heel and stalks back, hips swaying, to her place among the Drone camp.

I snarl under my breath, "Are you serious, Trey?"

"We'll deal with this later," he mutters. "For the record, it's over between me and her. It was just a fling. That was the loose end I was tying up yesterday."

I hit him with a disgusted look.

"Hey, Victoria," Presley calls across the divide. "You got any more boy-toys you need to offload? I've got room in my schedule."

"You couldn't handle my guys," Victoria snaps.

I crack up and Marcus snorts. He and Presley are dating now, but he's so laid-back that the exchange doesn't seem to bother him.

Presley saunters forward, her voluptuous curves swaying, and turns to the massive crowd. She extends her hands to her sides, radiating seduction, and quips, "Survey says?"

The crowd unleashes a torrent of cat calls, howls, and applause.

Presley shoots Victoria a smirk and returns to Marcus, curling around him suggestively.

Marcus grins and we all laugh.

Victoria tries to rally. "Fine, maybe Presley's got the it factor, but Melanie doesn't."

The crowd, in anticipation, shifts their collective gaze to me. I raise an eyebrow and decide to conceal my virginal status, still unknown to most at the school.

I cock a hip, run a seductive hand down Trey's chest, and purr in Victoria's direction, "I'm going to ride your toy into next Sunday, bitch."

Victoria's mouth drops open and her face turns crimson. She's been bested, and she knows it.

The crowd goes nuts, high-fiving and catcalling.

Trey turns his shocked eyes my way before squeezing them closed. "Oh my God," he murmurs seductively. "I love you, girl."

I raise an eyebrow and murmur back, "I love you too."

We stare at each other. Trey appears thrown by his admission of love and my response.

"Don't get all spun out now," I tell him. "Whatever this is between us works. We both knew we loved each other the second you grabbed my hand at the observatory. Just let it ride."

He opens his mouth to respond but is cut off by the growing energy of the crowd.

A chant begins and grows louder. "Fight! Fight! Fight! Fight!"

Joel steps forward and points in my direction, then glares threateningly at Trey. He's nearly manic as he bellows, "She's mine!" His hands are trembling, and he's radiating insanity. Unexpectedly, he lunges forward, making a grab for me.

Beside me, Trey growls, but I block any chance he has to step in.

I skirt Joel's advance, rushing under his outstretched arm. I whip around, running backward in my heels, giving me a clear view of my friends and the Drones. My back is to the crowd, but judging by their enthusiasm, they're on Team Mel.

I stop Joel dead in his tracks as I loudly yell, "How many girls have you raped, Joel?"

A hush falls over the crowd.

Joel's mouth drops open, and his friends look suddenly uncomfortable. For the benefit of the audience, I announce, "Joel tried to rape me after auditions last week." I point to my face. "That's where this came from. He gets off on torturing girls, and I'm not the first he's done this to."

Arch steps forward into the open space and demands of the crowd, "How many of you have been attacked by Joel?"

A collection of hands rises, and girls tear up all over the crowd. The guys in the crowd step to the front, radiating fury.

"Administration is aware and has done nothing!" Arch continues. "It's time *we* deal with this!" He turns to me. "Have at it, Melanie."

I surge forward, taking Joel off guard, and crack him square under the jaw with a perfectly landed battement kick. Joel is knocked off-balance and tumbles onto his side.

All that dance training has come in handy!

"And in heels, too!" Tanner exclaims. "Get it, girl!"

Once Joel has a chance to collect himself, he stares up at me in astonishment. I strut forward, aim my stiletto heel, and kick him in the gut as hard as I can.

He gasps and clutches his stomach.

With a yank, I roll him onto his back and kneel. Burning with vengeful anger, I tell him, "If you *ever* come near me again, it'll be the last damn thing you do. I'm not yours, Joel. You will never have me. I belong to Trey."

Joel's eyes shift to Trey, who says, "I don't care if I land in jail. If you threaten my girl again, you have my word your parents will have to bury you."

"The rest of the Drones are just as bad," I announce to the crowd, sweeping my arm in the direction of Joel's lackeys. "Have at it!"

The throng of students surges forward, and a full-scale brawl ensues.

Stan rushes me, and Trey steps in his path, hitting him with a right hook. Stan drops to the pavement. Trey turns to me. Battle lust pours in waves through our soulmate connection. I rush the few steps to him and hop up, wrapping my legs around his waist. He catches me, gripping my ribs, and kisses me passionately in the middle of the battlefield.

Fire shoots up both of our backs, and he growls, "Let's get the hell out of here."

I nod, ready to leave and find somewhere to be alone with Trey.

"Stop!" a voice bellows.

Our plan is halted, and everyone freezes midmotion.

Trey discreetly sets me down.

"The Drones are getting away!" Tanner yells.

The crowd surges in the direction Tanner indicates, but we're stopped by a wall of teachers, led by Principal Walker, who step up and block our path.

"Joel's made a habit of raping girls at this school," Arch tells Principal Walker. "Because the faculty refuses to handle it, we took the matter into our own hands."

The teachers look stunned and turn their heads to Principal Walker, who furrows his brow.

Faced with an angry mob of students, he announces, "You have my attention. I'm going to deal with this." He turns to Arch.

"How many in your group masterminded this early morning assault?"

Without hesitation, we all raise our hands. There's no point in folding on our gutsy display now.

Principal Walker gives a nod. "Arch's group, head to the conference room for a meeting. The rest of you get to class. The bell rang ten minutes ago."

We reclaim our backpacks and exchange pensive looks as the crowd disperses.

"Here goes nothing," Arch says.

CHAPTER *20*

We're all nervous as we walk down the hall toward the conference room.

"Let me and Arch handle this," I say.

The rest nod, and as we approach, Principal Walker steps into the hall.

His eyes widen as he scans the group. "Come in and have a seat," he says. He can't seem to help but chuckle. "You all look rather striking today."

We file into the room and sit down. Principal Walker, Arch, and myself claim the coveted spots at the head of the table.

The principal waits to speak until we're all seated. "I need you to fill me in. Please spare no details."

Arch gestures to me, and I take a deep breath.

"First, Principal Walker, I'd like to apologize for how rude I was during the fight last week. We've got a serious problem, but I didn't address you appropriately." I pause to collect my thoughts. "With that said, Joel Stamp and three of his student council friends tried to attack me again on Saturday night. This has to stop. There's something seriously wrong with Joel. Arch asked the crowd how many girls Joel has attacked, and the number of hands that went up was even more than we expected."

"I counted at least fifteen," Arch says.

Principal Walker leans back in his chair, considering what he has heard. "Well, kids. First of all, I'm sorry you got caught up in an altercation." He scans the faces around the table, his gaze eventually landing on mine. "Melanie, are you okay? I'm still in disbelief that Joel attacked you so viciously. Not just once, but twice."

"I'm fine, sir," I say, looking down. "Thanks." I close my eyes, draw another deep breath, and reach for Trey's hand.

Principal Walker sighs. "I'm sorry for not handling this differently the other day. Rest assured, I now realize that Joel is a serious problem. I promise I'll take any action necessary to have him expelled."

My shoulders relax, and I feel the tension leave my body.

"More than that," Walker continues, "though his father will likely have me strung up, I'll be calling the police as soon as this meeting is adjourned. I'll also be notifying campus security about the incident and giving them a list of students I plan to expel."

The group rumbles with approval.

I'm suddenly aware of the unlikely effectiveness of security officers in keeping the campus safe. I send a pulse to Trey through our connection, and he studies the bubble, his eyes a touch unfocused.

"No offense intended," Trey says, voicing our shared concern. "But your security officers can't even keep the gates guarded around here. How do you expect them to keep an eye out for a couple of kids in a student body of fifteen hundred?"

Principal Walker looks confused. "The security officers around here do a fine job. We don't even have much of a ditching problem."

One look around the room confirms we're all baffled by Principal Walker's ignorance of the daily comings and goings of the student population.

"You got that right," Tanner says with an enthusiastic nod. "No ditching problem here. It's impressive, really."

Everyone but Trey and I snicker, Tanner of course being the one to ditch more often than he goes to class.

Trey and I become lost in a worried mind-to-mind exchange. I send a bubble filled with my foreboding. I'm positive Joel can outsmart security. Even if he can't, I have to come and go from campus each day, leaving Joel all the opportunity in the world to plan another attack. Once he has been expelled, there's no telling how hyper focused on me he'll become. There's nothing really to stop him from trying again.

Trey sends back a bubble that he plans to walk me to my classes and drive me home from school every day.

I send back relief, and he exhales.

"I don't mean to sound shallow," Marcus says, "but the guys you're going to expel are the officers on the student council."

"Yeah," Finley says, worry creeping into her voice. "What does this mean for the dance? We're all really excited about it."

Principal Walker ponders this for a moment. Finally, he says, "All right, here's the deal. There's a procedure for this kind of situation. But these particular circumstances are challenging, as we've never had to remove an entire student council before. To be clear, I'm going to expel the students who attacked Melanie on Saturday night. The council members who weren't involved can't be expelled, but they will be removed from the council. Seems we'll need to start rebuilding the council from scratch." He sighs and continues. "I propose that I make an announcement and open the field to any who wish to run for president. The person elected to the position will, with my personal assistance and approval, assign his or her officer selections and student council members. Does that sound acceptable?"

Arch's eyes narrow.

"Uh-oh," Val says. "He's got that look."

We all hit Arch with curious eyes. He scans our faces, meeting each with consideration. Finally, he turns to Principal Walker. "I'm assuming a good council would be organized, well respected by the student population, have a decent GPA, and have kick-ass taste in activities and themes?"

We all glance around at each other as knowing grins spread on our faces.

"I'd like to put my name on the nomination list for student council president," Arch says.

Principal Walker's brow rises. After a moment, he nods. "Actually, Arch, that's not a bad idea. I think you would make a fantastic president. Your grades, and behavior, well, usually . . . are exemplary."

"Hey now, don't tell everyone!" Arch returns. "I've got a reputation to uphold."

We all laugh, and Principal Walker smiles.

"Yes, of course," he says. "You're a terrible problem. Okay then. It's settled. I'm going to require any prospective presidents to submit their names by sixth period today. I'll put your name on the submission list."

"I appreciate that, sir."

Principal Walker stands. "You kids head to the office for tardy slips. Melanie, please stick around a minute."

What in the world?

Everyone rises and heads out the door, while glancing back at me with worried expressions.

Trey grabs my hand, and I feel a pulse through our connection that he doesn't want to let me walk to class by myself. Joel and his thugs might be on their way to expulsion, but as far as we know, they may still be creeping around the school today. We have no clue where they slipped away to after the brawl.

"Trey, you should get to class," Principal Walker says.

"Sorry, sir," Trey says, "but I'm not leaving Melanie. I'm walking her to and from all her classes until the guys who attacked her are gone. No one's going to touch her again."

"Don't you think that will get in the way of your own attendance and studies?" the principal asks.

"Frankly, sir, if she's attacked again, you have my word that it'll get in the way of *everyone's* studies. I'll rain hell down on this place if anyone hurts her. For now, it's actually easier for me to just keep an eye out to avoid any potential problems. My grades are good, so I can take the tardy hit. I promise to fly below the radar, and it won't become a trend. What happened this weekend was . . ." He looks at me and pulls me in closer. "It was terrifying. I need to see to it that she's okay before I'll be able to focus on my classes."

Principal Walker purses his lips. "Very well. Don't look for trouble though, okay? Get her to class and then head to class yourself."

"Thank you, sir," Trey says.

I offer a tiny grateful smile to Principal Walker. It's good of him to make this exception to the school's strict tardy policy.

"Well then," Walker says. "That solves the problem I wanted to discuss with Melanie. I had a plan for security to escort her until this mess gets resolved, but it sounds like you've got it covered. Come to me if there are any issues."

CHAPTER *21*

I exit my third-period classroom to find Trey there waiting for me. He's leaning against a row of lockers and looking at his pager. He smiles when he sees me, clips the pager on his front pocket, then steps in to lift my chin to kiss me. A sea of students has to part around us because we're standing in the middle of the wide hallway.

He pulls away and whispers, "Today has been the longest day of my life. I need school to let out so we can go spend some time together."

I smile up at him. Any doubt I had that I'm his evaporates.

Trey glances down the hall behind me and frowns. I follow his gaze to Victoria and her Drones headed our direction. If looks could kill, I'd be dead.

Victoria picks up the pace, moving toward me with a vicious sneer. "Do you *seriously* think you're going to get away with this?" She stops in front of me and cocks a hip. "Even if you manage to get Joel expelled, student council is *ours*! Don't you know who we are?"

After Victoria storms off, Trey touches my arm. "Melanie, look at me."

I continue staring down the hall. Victoria is repulsive. Now that we're past the fight-fueled bravado from this morning, I find I have mixed feelings about the matter of Victoria and Trey. The thought of what Trey did with her makes me physically sick. We haven't yet had a conversation about our pasts, and I feel stupid for making the assumption that Trey wasn't any more experienced than me. The fact that some of his experience comes from being with Victoria . . .

"Please look at me," Trey says, a nervous edge to his voice.

I turn slowly to meet his eyes, knowing that even though I've never imagined feeling so connected to someone, I will happily leave him if it means avoiding Victoria.

"First," he says, "I'm sorry. I thought long and hard about whether to tell you about Victoria, and I decided against it. I'm not thrilled with myself for getting involved with her in the first place. It was a mistake, but it was something that happened before I met you."

I take a deep breath, look down, and collect my thoughts. "Can I ask you some things?"

"Of course," Trey says with a nod.

"Why the hell did you really see her yesterday? One last cheap throw?"

He cracks his neck as if trying to buy himself time. Finally, he says, "All we did was talk. I ended it, and that's the extent of it."

I feel like I just got dunked in a vat of ice water. "You really had a fling with her?" I do little to hide my disgust.

When Trey reaches for my hand, I pull back.

"Please don't touch me. The *last* thing I want is to feel your emotions about that sleaze."

He looks worried, perhaps frantic, but doesn't seem to know what to say.

"Obviously, you slept with her."

Trey rubs his forehead. "Yes. I've been hoping like hell that it wouldn't come up. But I can't change the past. I intended to cut things off when Adam called her out after school the other day, but there hasn't been time." His eyes are sad, and it's obvious he regrets being with her.

Still . . .

"I'm not a fan of what you've done with her. I wish we'd had this talk before now, if only because Victoria enjoyed telling me, in public, and I absolutely detest that. You know as well as anyone that she goes out of her way to torture me."

Trey cups my chin. "I'm sorry I gave Victoria the opportunity to win points in these nasty social Olympics you two have been competing in. I would like to point out though that, while it feels like we've been together forever, we only started dating less than forty-eight hours ago. With everything else going on, there really hasn't been much time to discuss any of this."

I stare at him, unsure how to respond. I decide to go with honesty. "You do make a good point. My brazen display aside, I'm going to level with you, because we don't really know each other all that well yet. The only other person I've ever gone on a date with, or kissed, is Adam."

"I sort of assumed you and he had done more than just kiss. I mean, he's gotten around with half the girls at this school."

"Not every girl's a skank, Trey. I get that that's what you're accustomed to." I gesture down the hall. "But some of us don't give it up on the first date."

Trey closes his eyes. After a moment, he opens them and says, "I apologize. I wasn't trying to imply any of that."

There's a sinking feeling in my stomach. "Do you still have a thing for her?"

"No," he says. "She has a good side, but I haven't seen it in a while. I hate to admit this, but I think it's better that I'm a hundred percent honest with you. My interest in Victoria was mostly physical."

"Wonderful," I huff. Of all the things he could be honest about, I wish he'd kept that one to himself.

He closes his eyes again and takes in a deep, slow breath. "Now I'm sorry I said it. Look, Melanie"—he opens his eyes and levels me with a sincere gaze—"I'm sorry. Victoria was a mistake. I'd take it back if I could, but I can't. You're the only girl I want. It's you and me, and that's it. I promise."

We stand in tense silence for what feels like a lifetime. Finally, I settle on a decision.

"The thought of you and Victoria makes me sick. She's a mean, nasty viper, and I hoped you'd have better taste than that. There's nothing we can do about it, though. I need to get to class." I turn on my heel and walk away, nervously watching for potential trouble.

— —

Mr. Bentley claps his hands to get our attention.

When the classroom door opens, a flash of fear surges through me. *What if one of the Drones has decided to spring an attack right here in the classroom?* When Tanner slips through the doorway, I exhale.

Calm down, Mel. There aren't enemies around every corner.

I scoff at the thought because the opposite has already proven true, and I have every reason to be on my guard. Still, I'm torn. On one hand, I hope the police that Principal Walker promised to call will arrest Joel. On the other, given his family's wealth and privilege, Joel is unlikely to stay locked up for long. It might be better to just take my chances that he learned his lesson from this morning's beatdown. I worry how enraged Joel might become if he's actually taken into custody. Either way, I'm in certain danger.

The loudspeaker hums to life, and Ms. Ferry's voice pitches staccato. "A big Hollywood High hello to you all this Monday afternoon! We have a series of important announcements. Your attention, please. First, the 1992 homecoming court results are in!"

Presley and I side-eye each other, and she grabs my arm. We're both hoping we made the court, but we'll be happy for whoever of us wins. My stomach knots with anticipation as Ms. Ferry, with her usual dramatic flair, announces the court by grade, starting with the senior class and working her way down. It's agony waiting for her to get to the freshman court. Finally, she says, "Your freshman homecoming prince is Marcus Vinsky. And, in a surprising turn of events, for princess we have a tie! Your freshman princess*es* are Presley Verelle and Melanie Slate!"

"Ready, steady, launch!" Tanner hollers, and the guys pelt Marcus with paper airplanes.

Presley and I dive under the table to avoid the aerial assault, laughing and squealing as we hug.

Marcus cracks up as he ducks and dodges the paper missiles. "No hard feelings, brother?" he asks Tanner.

"Not at all, man. I knew you'd win." Tanner grins and takes an animated bow. "It was an honor just to be nominated."

Now that the projectile coast is clear, the class gathers around our table. Hugs and high fives are passed around. As everyone heads back to their seats, Presley and I turn to each other and grin.

She fist-bumps me. "Hell yes! All I wanted was for one of us to beat Victoria, but *both* of us beating her? Even better!"

Our attention is returned to the announcements as Principal Walker's voice comes over the loudspeaker.

I move to the edge of my seat.

"Now that we have that behind us, ladies and gentlemen, Hollywood High School is currently preparing to hold a very special election. As some of you know, our student council has been disbanded due to unfortunate circumstances. Anyone interested in running for student body president needs to submit their intent no later than the beginning of sixth period. I apologize for the short time frame, but these are extraordinary circumstances, and the homecoming dance must be planned immediately. Only juniors and seniors are eligible for the position of president, and a GPA of 3.0 or higher is required for consideration. Thank you."

CHAPTER *22*

After the bell rings, Presley, Marcus, and I exit Mr. Bentley's classroom.

Waiting at the bottom of the stairs are Trey, Val, and Hiram. Trey's expression is serious, expectant. When I reach the bottom step, he hugs me, but whatever he's about to say is interrupted when his sister Kelsey approaches us, a kid named Chad who I've seen at school by her side.

"What's up, dude?" Chad claps hands with Trey and then brings him in for a shoulder pound. Chad looks me up and down. "Now I see what all the fuss is about. Dang, Trey. You've got a hell of a track record lately."

The air around us turns tense, but Trey laughs it off. He gets Chad in a headlock and gives him a noogie. "It's all right, guys," Trey says. "Chad and I have been friends since we were babies." He releases his old friend and shoots him a mock glare. "Don't make it worse, numb-nuts. I'm already in enough hot water as it is."

Kelsey and Val shift their attention my way. Val gives me an appraising look. Seems like there might be a conversation coming with the girls.

"If you ever want a real man," Chad jokes to me, "just let me know."

Everyone laughs.

"Good luck," Hiram tells him. "It's only been a couple of days, and those two can't even look at anyone else."

"So, you're the new big secret." Kelsey looks to Trey and raises an eyebrow. "A homecoming princess, huh?" She steps forward to hug me. "Trey filled us in on what happened. I'm glad you're okay." She pulls away, adding shyly, "Thanks for kicking Joel in the teeth this morning. I still have nightmares from what he tried to do to me."

I'm surprised how much Kelsey looks like Trey—same tan complexion, light-brown eyes, and raven-black hair. We don't know each other yet, but we're a part of the same unfortunate sisterhood, and I feel instantly protective of her.

With the reminder, my eyes dart right, then left, warily looking for Drone trouble.

"I'll catch you guys later," Trey says.

He pulls me aside, and we head to the benches across the quad.

When he congratulates me on winning homecoming princess, I guess I don't respond with the enthusiasm he was expecting because he quickly becomes serious again, his forehead creased with worry. "I am so sorry, Melanie. I promise there won't be any more nasty surprises."

The whole Victoria situation makes me uncomfortable. Sensing my misgivings, Trey pulls me in and hugs me.

"I appreciate that," I say quietly. "I think I just need a chill lunch with my friends."

Trey sighs. "Okay. I'll head to my usual spot with the varsity guys."

Curiosity gets the best of me. "Baseball?"

"Yep," Trey says with a grin. "Outfielder."

I smile, intrigued. "I didn't know that."

He laughs, shaking his head. "I think we've established that there's a lot we don't know about each other. Completely logical, given that we just met . . . in this lifetime, at least."

"A lot has happened in a short time," I concede. "I went from getting stood up by Adam to sending mind-to-mind messages with a varsity outfielder." I smirk playfully, adding, "Athletes aren't usually my thing, but"—my eyes cut to his muscled arms—"I'm reconsidering due to some unexpected perks."

Trey throws his head back and laughs, then hits me with a smoldering look, stating suggestively, "Your brand of flirtation is going to push me over the edge." He goes quiet for a moment, glancing to the side. "There's something important I want to discuss with you."

"I'm listening."

"Given how fast things are moving with us on a metaphysical level, and your earlier profession about your—for lack of a better way to put it—innocence, I'd like to take the physical stuff between us slow. I'm planning to intentionally pump the brakes. I don't want to lose you because this freight train hops the tracks and derails."

I can't help but smile, but then look down when a whisper of insecurity stirs inside. Maybe he isn't really interested in me in that way. I mean, if Victoria was appealing to him . . . she and I couldn't be more different—in most respects, anyway.

I continue staring at my feet.

Trey taps his finger lightly on my temple and holds out his hand. "Hey, let me in."

Hesitantly, I take his hand. He sends a bubble of inquiry about my thoughts. I look up, and my expression turns quizzical as curiosity sparks. While our minds are still linked, I locate and then lift a barrier—one that's so much a part of my natural psyche that it was invisible until now, like a secret passageway.

Trey's brow shoots up. "Interesting."

"Right? Apparently you can enter my mind and take a look around—if I allow you to, that is. In this case," I offer sheepishly, "I thought it might spare us the awkward conversation about how I'm worried you're not really that into me, given your slowing down of the physical stuff."

"Ah, I see," Trey says with a nod. "I'm happy to consider your concerns, of course. But the opposite is true. I'm way too interested."

Relieved, I exhale.

Still, as promised, he studies my thoughts on the matter, and then takes my hand, sending me a pulse that makes it clear how much he cares. He also assures that he's not using me for a backseat romp.

I send one back, stating that what he's sent matters to me, but out loud, I purr, "That's a shame."

He laughs and turns his head to the side, trying to regain control of his mind that's sputtering, thanks to my suggestive comment. Quietly, he says, "I've got my hands full with you, don't I?"

I smile and wink before rising to my feet and walking off, hips swiveling, to catch up with my friends.

Bear grabs my hand and pulls me into the middle of the tight friend circle. I glance over my shoulder at Trey before we round the corner. He gives me a wink, and I grin.

I catch Arch midsentence.

". . . and on top of that, there's safety in numbers. Joel and his Saturday Night Drones might have been expelled, but I saw a couple of their student council thugs when I was headed to fourth period. Some of them are still here. Keep your eyes open."

My mood shifts to one of dread, and I look around fearfully, expecting the Drones to attack at any moment. I sigh. *This is worse than avoiding Joel. Now I have to worry about that whole pack of thugs.*

CHAPTER *23*

Trey comes in unexpectedly and heads to Ms. Ferry, who's sitting at a table at the front of the auditorium. My sixth-period acting class is analyzing *Death of a Salesman*, and I'm not particularly enjoying the process. I watch as he kneels down and hands my teacher an office slip. Ms. Ferry nods and looks my way as Trey rounds the front of the audience seats and walks up the aisle toward me.

He leans over with a hand on the seat in front of me. "I'm springing you. Let's roll."

Presley, sitting next to me, raises a speculative eyebrow. "What for?" she asks on my behalf.

Trey slides an amused glance to Presley. "Because she's living rent-free in my head, she's irritated at me over the Victoria issue, and I'm beyond distracted needing to get her alone so I can slide my hands up her back while she kisses me."

Presley grins at me and hisses, "Hot."

"What was the slip you just gave to Ms. Ferry?" I ask.

"A nurse's office slip," Trey says slyly. "I have a whole backpack full of them. My sister is the TA in the copy room."

I laugh and toss my stuff in my backpack before slinging it over my shoulder.

"You don't feel good, by the way," Trey says.

I let my face fall with some pitiful feigned illness and grab at my stomach. Trey's back is to Ms. Ferry, who's watching us across the distance.

When Trey chuckles, I bat at his arm,

"Your shoulders are shaking," I whisper. "No laughing at my life-and-death illness." To screw with him, I set a hand to my forehead and, with a heavy sigh, pretend to feel faint.

Trey's shoulders shake harder. "You theater kids are nuts."

He puts an arm around my shoulder and shuttles me across the auditorium. He stops me at the door and scans the expansive view from the top of the four-story staircase that runs along the outside of the building. Satisfied that we're safe from potential Drone attacks, Trey holds his hand out to me. I take it and close the propped-open door behind us.

I back up, lean against the big metal door, and pull him to me. He smiles suggestively and puts his hands on either side of my shoulders. I slide my hands under his tank top and let them rest on his back. "Is kissing out of the question," I whisper, "in this annoying purity pact of yours?"

He leans down, his lips almost touching mine, and whispers back, "You're trouble, girl."

"I really am," I murmur. "Good luck holding on to your resolve."

He crushes his lips against mine, and my mind tunnels down a hormonal rabbit hole. By the time he pulls away, my head is spinning.

To my surprise, Trey's not in any better shape.

"This soulmate connection makes things a lot more intense," he says. "I'm going to have a hell of a time keeping things PG." He cups my chin. "I want you to understand, though, that it's important to me."

I let out a sigh. "For the record, I'm not planning to argue. But for the sake of clarity, I am curious as to why."

Trey looks me in the eye. "I've made mistakes before, believing others were special. The second I met you, I realized I was wrong about previous girls. I tend to move fast, and I don't want to do that this time. This soulmate bond between us deserves time and consideration."

My heart beats harder, and I hold up my hand, unable to speak for fear I might tear up. Trey takes my hand, and I send a pulse of how much it means to me that he cares enough about handling us the right way. *Frankly, I always thought teenage boys were heartless trolls. Trey legitimately seems different.*

He catches that last part—that I didn't intend to send—and it makes him laugh. He answers, "Actually, we are, but, where you're concerned, I'm determined not to be. I'm not going to screw this up."

We descend the stairs, but I'm wary. I've spent the entire day worried about the Drones and the constant anxiety is wearing on me.

"Relax, Melanie," Trey says. "I'm watching for trouble. I'm not going to let anything happen to you. I've got a reputation among the Regulars that rivals Adam's with the Magnets. There's a reason he involved me when he first confronted Joel."

When we reach the bottom of the stairs, I slip my arm around Trey's waist and settle in under his arm. I decide to enjoy our stroll. "I'm guessing Adam's regretting that choice about now."

Trey chuckles. "I think you're right. I'm glad he involved me, though. It sped up my meeting you. I already knew there was something about you."

"You too. I kept noticing you."

"I feel like I've known you forever," Trey says. "You're as committed to me as I am to you, right?"

I stop, stunned by his sudden insecurity. "I don't date much, Trey. Frankly, I usually think guys are more trouble than they're worth. Adam certainly proved me right there. If this wasn't something special, you and me, I wouldn't bother. The Victoria situation's a big deal, though. I do not enjoy being blindsided by a bimbo."

He runs his hand over my right arm, takes a deep breath, and lets it go as he contemplates my words. His gaze is penetrating and serious. "I'm not going anywhere, Melanie. We've got some talking to do, obviously. It's a lot. We're a lot. But, this"—the energy pulses through our hands—"scares me. You're the one." He laces his fingers with mine. "I love you."

"I love you too." I flash him a wide smile. "This is batshit crazy."

Trey laughs, and we head off on our walk. We pass Victoria and her vipers, who glare at us, but we make a point to avoid eye contact.

"Trey!" Victoria calls out.

Trey mutters under his breath, "Nope."

A smile, a touch sinister, spreads across my face. I stop and look up at Trey.

He runs his fingers down my arms, making me shiver. He then hooks a finger in the waistband of my skirt and tugs me to him before sliding his hands around my waist and kissing me. After the kiss ends, we linger, our lips still tantalizingly close. I side-eye Victoria, who rushes off, her eyes flooded with tears.

As we round the corner of the Commons building, the loud-speaker system clicks on. We stop to listen as Principal Walker's voice echoes through school grounds.

"Good afternoon. I have an update to share regarding the status of our student council election. I'm pleased to announce that this is going to be a rapid process because we've had only one submission for president. I believe most of you know him. Our new student body president is Arch Terani."

I turn to Trey with a satisfied smile. "He did it!"

We join in the collective cheer that can be heard throughout school grounds.

The bell rings, and students rush from every classroom around us. Trey is instantly wary and on alert. That many students converging in one place could easily hide trouble. He puts a firm hand on the back of my neck and steers me the direction of the faculty parking lot, which isn't as congested, and we move along at a brisk clip.

"You're making me nervous," I say.

"Don't be. Two of my brothers are Los Angeles police officers, and my dad, before he retired in June, used to own a private security company, specializing in personal bodyguard detail for public officials and celebrities."

I glance at him, surprised.

"My dad trained me well," he says. "I take no chances. That's how I was able to see just how useless the security guards around here are. I was impressed how you had that figured out this morning."

"They're a joke," I say.

"I suppose then it goes without saying that I'm handling you myself for a reason."

We make our way around the backside of the furthest bungalow in Actors' Alley, where the group is gathered around our usual lunch table.

"Hang here with us," Hiram says as we join them. "Arch is in a meeting with Principal Walker. He'll be out shortly with details."

Before we can sit down, Adam approaches us. "Can we talk for a second?" he asks me.

I grab Trey's hand and send a bubble, asking if he's okay with this.

He nods with a shrug and returns a message that he trusts me.

I give his hand a squeeze before letting go and following Adam to a spot at the base of the theater staircase.

He turns to me. "What's up with you and Trey?"

"A lot," I reply, keeping my answer intentionally vague. What's happening between me and Trey isn't something I feel comfortable sharing with Adam. Hell, I'm still working to get a grasp on this soulmate stuff myself.

Adam looks down at me, his eyes sincere. "I want you to know that I'm truly sorry about the other night. I wasn't trying to play you, and I don't want it in your head that you fell for a line."

I don't know what to say.

"I don't suppose there's any chance you'd give me another shot?"

I'm done with Adam, but curiosity gets the best of me. "What about Valerie?"

He shakes his head. "All we do is fight. She's beautiful and intriguing, but damn is she confrontational." He glances at Val, sitting at the table, and looks back at me. "I screwed up, Melanie."

Trey's watching me with guarded curiosity. "You okay?" he mouths.

I nod and, while still gazing at Trey, say to Adam, "I appreciate that. I do. But I've found my guy. I love Trey. He's it for me. I'm off the market."

When Arch emerges from his meeting with Principal Walker, we cross back to the group. As curious as I am to hear the latest, the distraction of Trey proves formidable. When I get to him, my mind is carried a million miles away. He smiles at me, laces a hand with mine, and cups my jaw with the other hand. He then leans his forehead against mine and sends a pulse about what Adam wanted.

I send him back the details.

Trey whispers just loud enough for me to hear, "You sure I don't have competition?"

I shake my head, rise on my toes, and wrap my arms around his neck. "You'll never have competition."

He smiles, leaning in, and kisses me.

My head spins—in the best possible way. *I'm never going to get sick of this.*

Our private world is interrupted by Arch, stating loudly, "Did you catch all of that, Trey and Melanie?"

We turn to him, flustered, and Trey responds, honestly, "Nope. Not one bit."

The group laughs.

"We need to meet on Saturday," Arch says. "Student council."

Trey shrugs. "My practice ends at one. Anything after that works for me."

"Just a thought," Tanner says, "but Melanie's told me she has a pool. If we do the meeting there, we can have a pool party after!"

Everyone clamors excitedly, begging me to make it happen.

"You know," Hiram says, "we *are* due for a party."

Trey discreetly runs a hand down my back, and I temporarily lose track of my thoughts. *Every time he touches me, my brain seems to leak out my ear.*

Arch is at the tail end of a statement when I realize he's talking to me.

". . . and find out, Melanie."

I gesture with my hand from Trey to my ear. "Yeah, I got none of that. Say again?"

CHAPTER 24

Trey slides into the driver's seat of his car and closes the door. We sit for a moment in silence before he pulls out of the parking lot. I have no clue where we're headed, but it really doesn't matter. I just want time alone with him.

"Student council sounds like a lot," he says.

"It *really* does." I glance at my boyfriend. "Think we can quit?"

He laughs. "Arch would kill us."

Trey's energy shifts serious. "Melanie, what happened today is really nagging at me." He takes his eyes off the road for a moment and turns to me. "I didn't want to start things off like that." His expression is shadowed with regret.

I sigh and loll my head in his direction. "Can we let it go? I got to publicly insult Victoria, I kicked Joel in the face, and he ran off with his tail between his legs. After all that, this whole thing with your ex seems kind of ridiculous, especially when we have the Drones to worry about. I can get over it if you can."

He belts a sarcastic laugh. "Well, thank you. I wasn't going to be able to sleep tonight from worrying about our squabble. But now I can look forward to a sleepless night because of Joel trying to hunt you down and rape you." His expression washes over with vulnerability. "My biggest fear is losing you because I do something stupid. Now I get to panic about you getting hurt."

I unzip my backpack and pull out my Discman. "I might be able to eliminate one of your worries. So, I love music. I know this probably isn't your thing, but can I play you a song?"

He nods, his expression genuinely curious.

I pop the homemade CD out of my Discman and hand it to him. "Number four."

He slips the disc into the car player and skips forward. The sultry pull of the music hums from the speakers.

"This has been my favorite song since I was a kid."

"What is it called?"

I smile nostalgically. "'Blue Jean Blues,' but I only like the Jeff Healey version."

He glances at me but doesn't say anything, letting the music talk.

"When I was little," I say after a time, "I actually thought the song was about someone losing a pair of blue jeans."

Trey chuckles.

"It's not, of course," I say. "It's about someone finding the one person that makes them comfortable in their own skin." I take a breath, a little overwhelmed, and, with misty eyes, I glance Trey's way. "Everything else aside, I knew you were the one for me because love with you feels like this song sounds."

When he doesn't respond, my insecurity surfaces. "Tell me what you're thinking."

Trey holds his hand out to me, and I take it. The pulse between us thrums.

He sends a surge of emotion, laced with love, through our connection. In the center is a mix of relief that he found me, and fear that he's going to lose me. I close my eyes and lean back against the headrest as his emotion bubble bursts in my chest and spreads through me.

While we're still drifting through the shared sensation, Trey pulls over onto an overlook on Mulholland and puts the car in park. He climbs out of the car and skirts the front end before opening my door and helping me out. He leans past me with a smile to turn up the volume on the stereo. He holds out his hand and I take it, looking at him curiously.

What is he doing?

He answers my unspoken question by setting my hands on his shoulders. When we start dancing, I can't help but giggle. This is the last thing I expected.

He smiles. "That was hands down the *girliest* sound I've heard you make. You're usually tough as nails."

"What can I say? You bring out my girly side. I suppose that's because I feel safe with you. I don't have to be tough or worry about anything."

"That means a lot," he says with a soft smile. "That's exactly how I want you to feel. In truth, being with someone as independent as you makes me wonder if you even need me."

The music builds.

He takes my hand, spinning me twice before pulling me back in. He holds my hips and rolls me into a backbend. I'm flexible enough from dance that I nearly fold in half before he snaps me back up, his hands firmly on my hips as he draws me back to him.

His expression holds equal parts heat and amusement.

"What?" I ask with a smile.

He shakes his head.

Playfully, I hold up my hand and reach for his. "I'll get it out of you one way or another."

He belts surprised laughter. "I was just thinking you were bendy. The rest of the thought wasn't exactly polite. A good time, though."

After feigning an offended look, I break into laughter.

Our energy shifts, matching the heat in his expression.

He stops dancing and slides his hands around my lower back, pulling me against him. He rests his forehead against mine. "I love you."

I slip my hand between us, set it on his chest, and send a pulse. "I love you too."

His eyes close, and he inhales deeply.

He takes a moment to study the message. It's complicated, but it boils down to me feeling whole with him.

Finally, Trey opens his eyes. He brushes his lips against mine, whispering, "I'm going to marry you one day." He kisses me, and our energy spreads, filling all the parts of me that have been insecure for years.

My heart squeezes, and I hop up, wrapping my legs around him.

He catches me easily, all while our kiss rages on. His hands tighten on my back, and I gasp against his lips. Things escalate, unexpectedly, and he turns and sets me down on the hood of his car. He moves back just enough to put a little breathing room between us and stares into my eyes. "I swear to you that I'll never touch another girl again because nothing compares to this thing between us."

The moment is interrupted by the rumble of a nearby car. Distracted, we hadn't noticed the late-eighties Honda Accord now idling roughly fifteen feet away.

Joel stares at us through the windshield and revs the engine.

"Get in the car," Trey orders.

I hop down as Trey slides over the hood to the driver's side door. Together, we jump in the car. With the engine running, Trey throws the Z28 into gear and hits the gas.

Dirt and gravel fly as he cranks the wheel right, and we turn to face Joel.

Joel revs the compact sedan, and I can't help but laugh because I know what's coming. Trey grins, puts the Camaro in park, and revs the engine. The American muscle car roars its challenge, and the difference between the two engines is comical. Joel's mouth drops open, and Trey and I laugh.

"Buckle up," Trey says. "Time to teach this asshole a lesson."

When Joel pulls out onto the winding road, Trey holds back for just a moment before gunning the engine and trailing him. We make it through four dramatic curves before Trey abandons the chase, turns the Camaro around, and heads in the direction of my house.

I glance his way. "It might sound weird to say, but I'm torn between being scared of Joel and feeling sorry for him. I mean, it's kind of pathetic, right? Him following me around like this?"

Trey shakes his head. "Don't let him fool you, Mel. The guy is sick, and dangerous. Don't drop your guard for even a moment. I need you to stay aware."

CHAPTER *25*

When the doorbell rings, I take one last look around. Rich has placed bunches of red and black balloons in every corner of the living room and dining room. I can't help but laugh. My parents are thrilled about this new student council turn of events and took to the idea of the pool party far better than I expected.

"Rich, you realize we're not little kids anymore, right?"

"*Everyone* likes balloons!" So typically Rich. "I guarantee every kid will go home with one."

We shall see.

Mom has placed bowls of chips, popcorn, M&M's, and fruit trays on each table. She's currently in the kitchen with lunch prep well underway. It's clear that both of my parents are enthusiastic and nervous about getting to know my new friends.

I open the front door to a sea of smiling faces. Everyone flows in, chatting excitedly. It looks like Rich was right because Finley squeals when she sees the balloons.

"Can I take one home?" Marcus asks.

I shake my head incredulously, and Rich gives me a look that says, "Told you so."

"Yes, Marcus," I say with a laugh. "*Please* take home a balloon. My stepfather is convinced you're all going to want one."

"For Pops," Adam says, walking through the door. "I'll tie a balloon to the handlebars of my Harley and drive the whole way home with it." He pats Rich on the shoulder.

Adam is the last to make his way inside, and I close the door behind him. My parents still have a soft spot for Adam, even though he stood me up.

Rich grins at him. "Good to see you again, Adam."

The others introduce themselves to my parents and thank them for hosting. We make small talk for a time before Arch claps his hands, calling us to order, and we gather in the living room.

"We have a lot of work ahead of us," Arch says. "First things first. Val, where are we with the location and deejay?"

Trey stands and holds out his hand to me. We head into the den, where Rich looks up from the show he's watching.

He smiles our way. "Hey, kids." Something about Trey's cautious expression appears to concern him, and he asks, "What's wrong?"

Trey clears his throat. "As you know, Melanie's having issues with Joel Stamp, from school." Rich nods, and Trey continues, "I need you to keep an eye out. He drives a late-eighties gold Honda Accord. We have reason to believe he's hell-bent on raping Melanie. He's got a nasty history."

Rich's eyes widen. "You think this is that serious?"

Trey nods. "I need you to triple check every door lock and window. Please keep your eyes peeled for any signs of trouble." Trey glances my way. "I'm beyond worried that something will happen at night, or at the bus stop in the morning. Those are the only times I'm not there to keep an eye on her."

"How do you know all of this, Trey?" Rich looks Trey over curiously. "You're only sixteen, right?"

"I am sixteen, but I've got training most people don't. Long story short, until my dad retired a few months ago, he used to run his own personal security business. If baseball doesn't work out for me, I plan to reopen the business after I graduate. I used to work for him. When my dad booked a young celebrity client, I was put on their detail as the person physically closest to them in a crowd. Publicists and agents don't exactly like to see hulking, middle-aged bodyguards in publicity shots." Trey shrugs. "I blended in."

Rich's eyebrows furrow. "The fact that you actually know what you're talking about scares me even more."

"It should," Trey returns. "Joel is obsessed. If I had my way, I'd stay here, or Mel would stay at my house until this is all over. My very conservative mom would never allow her to stay with me, though."

"I don't think we're at that point yet, Trey. You have my word that I'll check every window and every door each night."

Trey nods, thanking him, and shuttles me back into the living room. We arrive and take a seat just in time for my part of the meeting.

"So far, so good," Arch says. "Let's switch to Melanie and the decoration team. What are you thinking, Mel?"

All eyes turn my way.

I take my notebook off the table and flip through the pages. "The decorations team met with Mr. B. We're allowed to start decorating the ballroom at ten in the morning on Saturday. The dance starts at seven, and it's going to be a tight squeeze getting everything set up in time for us all to get ready and arrive back at six to meet with the teacher chaperones. That's my main concern."

Rich, delivering a giant bowl full of chips, strides into the living room. "Hey, Carol," he calls into the kitchen, "come in here a minute. I have an idea to help the kids."

Mom appears a moment later, her hands covered in flour.

"Mel says they won't have much time after decorating the ballroom on Saturday to go home and get ready before they have to report back at the Roosevelt," Rich explains. "How about we get two hotel rooms—one for the boys and one for the girls—and get all the kids' stuff organized so they can just run upstairs after they decorate and get ready there?"

The room fills with the murmurs of excitement.

"Are you serious?" Presley says. "You'd do that for us?"

Rich looks from face to face. "Well, yeah! You don't think we'd leave you hanging, do you?"

The girls hop off the couch and hug Mom and Rich.

"You guys really are amazing," Arch says. "Thanks." Arch raises a tentative hand. "We're having a party at my and Hiram's house the night before the dance. As far as I'm concerned, everyone's got the green light to stay over. Then we can all head over to the Roosevelt together."

I look at Mom and Rich expectantly. "Can I stay?"

Mom looks unsure. "I don't know." Her eyes flicker Trey's way, and he gives her an innocent look. "Would it be okay if I called your parents to get a feel for things?" she asks Arch.

Arch scrunches up his face. "You can call them, but it might not help. Hiram's parents own the house that we rent, but we live on our own."

Mom's eyes widen. "Live on your own? You're still in high school."

"I know it sounds crazy," Arch says. "But I've been working since I was thirteen. Hiram too. Together we have enough saved to afford the place for the duration of high school, thanks to Hiram's folks giving us such a great deal. Being roommates has worked out great. Our families live too far out of town to commute daily to Hollywood High, but they didn't want us to sacrifice the opportunity to attend the school."

Rich and Mom exchange a surprised glance.

I'm just as stunned as they are. How do Arch and Hiram manage such an adult responsibility? Even with reasonable rent, their bills can't be easy to pay, especially in this town. These friends of mine are so far ahead of me it's mind-boggling.

Finally, Rich turns to Trey. "You'll stay there too and make sure she's okay?"

"Absolu—"

"Wait! Wait just a minute now." Adam gives Mom a wink. "No funny business. That's Carol's number one rule."

I roll my eyes and give him an exasperated look. "Can it, Adam. Don't blow up my spot."

"Yup, Adam's right," Mom says, sliding a mischievous glance at Trey and me. "No funny business."

Adam narrows his eyes at Trey, clearly proud of himself for stirring up trouble.

I side-eye Adam and coyly say to my mom, "You have my word that there will be nothing funny about our business."

Adam looks irritable as he glares at Trey.

"Suddenly the guy's a paragon of virtue," Trey mutters under his breath.

After she and Rich agree to let me stay at Arch and Hiram's, I finish my summary about the decorations. I pause, nervous about sharing the next bit. I've been mulling it over, and I think it's cool, but it'll be embarrassing if the others don't agree. "So, I had an idea that I wanted to run past you all. You might think it's dumb, but . . ."

"It's a good idea, Mel," Trey says. "They'll like it."

Everyone leans forward in their seats, alight with curiosity.

"Well . . . the dance is celebrity themed, so I contacted a local talent agent, and found out that, for five hundred dollars, we can hire six actors to stand at the entrance taking photos for the first two hours, playing like they're the paparazzi. We could do a whole red carpet deal, using the velvet ropes from the school's theater storage. You know, make everyone feel like they're real movie stars. Then we can position the professional photographer at the end of the red carpet, so the students can have their official pictures taken—which they can purchase later—as they're heading into the dance. I already talked to a local photographer, and he put together a sample package and flyer for the council to approve. . ."

My voice trails off.

No one has said a word, and I'm sure my idea has bombed.

Arch takes the flyer, and the rest of the group leans over to check it out.

Presley jumps to her feet. "Yes! Mel, it's genius! Everyone's going to buy pictures. It's a perfect fundraiser."

Relief washes over me.

"I can paint a replica of the Hollywood sign for the photo backdrop," Hiram says. "It'll be awesome."

"I want a picture with my best friends and the Hollywood sign," Finley says. "People are going to love this!"

"Great work, Mel," Arch says, patting my back.

Finley is frantically writing notes on a sheet of paper. Tanner takes out a pen and begins a list for her in his notebook.

"Well, that all sounds like a plan," Arch says. "It's going to be a busy week. I suggest we add red and black balloons to that list. I like the look of these. We can space out bunches of them along the ballroom walls, and put some at the entrance to the red carpet. Carol, can Finley get the information of the balloon place?"

Mom nods and ducks into the kitchen.

"Does anyone have anything else for today's agenda?" Arch asks.

Val raises her hand. "I brought poster board, red shiny letters, stars, and markers. After lunch, we need to make some posters advertising the dance to hang in the halls first thing Monday. Ms. Ferry can do an announcement first period. That'll get ticket sales rolling. Can everyone help me make the posters? We need thirty of them."

We all nod.

Mom returns with a slip of paper and hands it to Finley. "Sounds like you guys have things all figured out," she says. "Now, why don't you all head out back and have some fun. Pool's open. I'll have lunch ready in twenty minutes."

She doesn't have to tell us twice. Whooping and hollering, we're all on our feet and out the back door.

CHAPTER *26*

The backyard is buzzing with conversation, and the pool resembles a resort. The waterfall flows delicately into the deep end, and a steady breeze carries the scent of mom's flowers.

I remove my shirt and leggings, revealing my bikini underneath, and drop them in a pile next to my flip-flops. I could use a little time in the sun. I slip on my sunglasses, and lie down on my towel, grateful the weather is still so warm.

The moment I close my eyes, I hear Darren say to Trey, "You're one lucky dog."

Trey chuckles, and I turn red.

I can feel the stares of the other guys.

Shading my eyes, I look up to Presley and Val, standing to my right, and smack Presley on the leg. "Hey, can you two get into your swimsuits so those heathens have someone other than me to drool over?"

"I'll race you," Val says to Presley. "First one to the deep-end wall wins."

They slip off their shorts and shirts and dive into the pool in their swimsuits. Val is a good four inches taller than Presley, but

Presley swam competitively for years and quickly streaks ahead of her. Presley wins by a hand and comes up out of the water with a gasp.

She hoists herself up onto the edge of the pool and reaches for the weighted square game. "Boys!" she calls out, "finish stuffing your faces and take off those shirts. I want a show."

We whoop and holler as the boys do as commanded, and Presley surveys Marcus appreciatively.

"Let's see who wins," she says. "Anyone up for a dive game?"

Adam, Tanner, Trey, and Kenji all step up to the pool.

"No fair!" Tanner says. "Kenji's so tall he won't even have to dive in to reach them at the bottom."

Kenji waggles his eyebrows at Tanner. "Hey, you gotta give me the occasional pass. The negatives far outweigh the positives. I can never find pants that fit, and I smack my forehead on nearly every doorway at school."

Tanner laughs at him, smacking Trey in the stomach.

Trey doubles over, laughing from the hit, and the two begin to roughhouse.

Presley, looking like a *Baywatch* beauty in her black one-piece, holds up the weighted blocks. "Here we go." She tosses the blocks in one at a time. "On your marks, get set, go!"

The four guys dive in and snatch up as many blocks as they can. I sit up and watch as they each emerge and dump their blocks on the side of the pool.

It's clear Adam has the most points. "Yes!" he shouts.

He's too busy being cocky to notice that the other guys have him surrounded. As he opens his mouth to cry out again in victory, they cup their hands in front of them and blast Adam with a wave of water. He sputters, laughing, and chases them around the pool. They're like a bunch of little kids, and I can't help but be charmed. Sometimes it's hard to believe that our big tough guys can transform so easily into third-graders when it's just us.

Hiram swims over to the shallow end, wades up the stairs, and snatches a towel from the table a few feet away from me.

"You okay?" I ask him.

He nods. "Yup. I'm just gonna grab my boombox out of the trunk of my car. We need music, and I've got some new CDs."

The girls all grin at each other because Hiram has a music collection that could rival any professional deejay.

"Look out, Kelsey," Finley says. "Because this party's about to heat up."

Kelsey smiles at her. Val and Presley settle on the towels next to us.

"I haven't thanked you girls yet," Kelsey says. "So much about my life has changed recently. I'm so grateful you've accepted me into your group." She looks down and then back up with a sad expression. "I have a question for you . . ."

We all look at each other, concerned.

"Okay," Val says. "What's up?"

"Well," Kelsey says shyly, "I've seen how close you four are with your boyfriends. Melanie and Trey are going to end up married, I'm sure of it. Valerie and Adam can't keep their hands off each other. Presley and Marcus are the 'it' couple of the school. Tanner and Finley are adorable . . ." She trails off, wringing her hands.

"Kelsey, what's wrong?" Presley asks. "Is it you and Arch?"

We glance to the pool, where Arch is tossing a water football back and forth with Bear. He seems happy. Then again, Arch is always in a good mood.

"It's just that . . . he's not very affectionate," Kelsey explains. "Sometimes he holds my hand, and he always carries my backpack, but I don't think he's as into me as your guys are into you, you know?"

Valerie leans in. "I've known Arch a long time. I know for fact that he's a lot more into you than he lets on. He's just old-fashioned. In Arch's mind, he thinks he's being chivalrous when he avoids physical affection."

Kelsey tilts her head. "Would you think less of me if I said that he's respecting me to death?"

We all crack up.

Presley rolls over onto her back. "Maybe you need to make the first move."

"You think?"

"Definitely."

"All right." Kelsey gets to her feet and adjusts the top of her cute red bikini. "Game on."

Her tan skin glows in the sun as she strolls toward the pool. One by one, the guys are distracted from their game and turn to stare appreciatively at the bold new Kelsey.

Well, all except Trey, who glares at his sister and exclaims, "What the . . ."

We exchange a devilish look as Arch's eyes widen and his mouth falls open.

"Yes, girl," Presley says just loud enough for the rest of us girls to hear. "Go get him."

Kelsey steps onto the pool stairs and slowly wades down into the water. Arch watches in disbelief as Kelsey disappears under the pool's surface.

We all watch, transfixed, as the streak of tan and red bolts through the water.

"Hey, Arch!" Presley calls to him. "Incoming!"

Kelsey pops up in front of Arch. She smiles, wraps her arms

around his neck, and kisses him passionately.

All the guys say, "Ooooh," in unison like a bunch of fifth graders.

We lean forward, waiting for Arch's reaction.

When Kelsey ends the kiss, Arch slowly breaks into a smile.

"Well, hello, Kelsey," he says. "To what do I owe the pleasure?"

Kelsey, seemingly unfazed by everyone watching and listening in, says, "I appreciate the whole nice-guy routine, Arch. But I'm ready for us to step it up."

Arch's smile grows wider. "Whatever you say, boss." He wraps his arms around Kelsey's waist and kisses her again.

The girls all cat call.

"Yes!" Presley howls out. "Give him hell, Kelsey!"

Hiram reappears and sets his boombox down on the table. "Who's ready to party?" he says as "Motownphilly" by Boyz II Men booms out. "I bet I know a couple girls who'd like to dance."

He steps over and stretches out his hands, luring us girls off our towels. We hop up and surround him, dancing and laughing.

"I'm in heaven," he says, lifting his arms into the air.

The rest of the guys hoist themselves out of the pool and don't bother to dry off. It doesn't take long before our dance party is in full swing.

Trey dances his way to me and takes my hand. He spins and dips me, then pulls me back up and into a slow dance, even though the song has a fast, driving beat.

Over Trey's shoulder, I spot Kelsey and Arch kissing at the edge of the group.

I nudge Presley beside me and point to the newly supercharged couple. "Sometimes a girl just needs to embrace her inner Presley."

Presley grins.

CHAPTER 27

Early Monday morning, I run to catch up with my friends as they're making their way down the alley toward the school.

"My bus got here early," I say. "I can help put up posters."

When I don't get a response, a sense of dread creeps up my spine. "What's going on?"

Arch stops the group and clears his throat. "I just saw Trey sitting in the back booth at Snow White's."

"So?"

"He was with Victoria."

Fear and confusion start a war in my head. It feels like my heart might stop. "What do you mean?"

My friends look worried—all except Presley, who's radiating rage.

"If that asshole thinks he can two-time you," she says, "he's got another thing coming."

"Who has another thing coming?"

Adam's voice comes out of nowhere, making me jump. He approaches the group, flanked by Hiram and Tanner.

Arch fills them in, while I stare at the ground, willing myself not to cry.

"No way," Adam counters. "I don't know what's going on, but I'm sure there's a good explanation. There's zero chance Trey's cheating on Melanie." Though he speaks out in Trey's defense, there's hopefulness in Adam's voice.

I draw a ragged breath and look up, tears filling my eyes.

Finley puts an arm around my shoulder as I struggle to wrap my mind around what's happening.

"There's no way, Mel," Hiram says. "I know it looks bad, but there has to be an explanation."

Arch takes the lead, and together we head up Highland Avenue—toward Snow White's Café.

We walk in tense silence. My hands are trembling at my sides.

"This isn't happening," I say.

Presley slips her arm through mine. "If it is, I'll kill him."

"I feel bad that we're having to deal with this right now. We're supposed to be hanging the posters for the dance. The bell's going to ring any minute."

"To hell with the posters," Valerie says. "We can put them up later."

"Okay, out with it," Finley says to me. "How much do you know about Victoria and Trey?"

I sigh. "Just what all of you heard when Victoria announced to the world about going parking with Trey on Mulholland."

Kelsey drops back from Arch's side. "Actually, they dated all summer," she says. "It got pretty serious. Thing is, I thought they were still together, and then suddenly he was with you."

My mouth falls open. "You mean they *dated* dated?"

Kelsey shrugs. "He didn't tell you?"

I blink back a fresh round of tears. "He alluded to it being a fling."

"I can't stand that girl," she says, shuddering. "She was at our house every damn day. They were—" Kelsey stops herself, looking suddenly unsure.

"What?" I ask, coming to a stop. "Tell me."

Kelsey hesitates, then sighs. "They were inseparable. I'm sorry, Melanie, but, for whatever reason, my brother is downplaying their relationship."

Presley spits out a string of acid-tinged cuss words. "I'm so mad I can't see straight. What was he thinking? Victoria's a viper."

We cross the street at Hollywood and Highland.

My heart pounds as Snow White's Café looms closer.

"I know what he was thinking," Val says. "She's gorgeous, and she's got a reputation for being easy. I know we all thought there was no way Trey would ever get involved with her, but when it boils down to it, he's a guy."

When we get to the café door, Arch stops and looks back at me. "Before you jump to conclusions, give him a shot. Hear him out."

"Trey's got a reputation as a pretty good guy," Adam says, to my surprise. "He isn't a player."

Adam holds the door for me and the other girls, and the boys follow us into the long, narrow building. I stop ten feet from the back booth, and I'm suddenly red-hot mad.

Finley stops beside me and gasps.

"What the hell?" I growl through gritted teeth.

Trey doesn't hear me because he's entirely consumed with Victoria. Their backs are to us, and Trey's arm is around Victoria's shoulder. She's snuggled into him, their faces only inches apart, whispering intimately.

Like a secretary flipping frantically through a Rolodex, I roll through the stages of grief—denial, anger, bargaining, depression, acceptance—then begin again, this time stopping at anger. *Yup, rage it is!* I draw a shaky breath as the vicious version of Melanie, the one I keep clamped down most of the time, roars to the surface. "Trey!" I bark, loud enough for the entire restaurant to hear.

With a start, he turns to me, his eyes registering shock.

I take a step closer. "You want to explain why you're snuggling with the Evil Dead?"

"Tori, I need to go."

Trey's attempt to scoot out of the booth is thwarted when the group of us moves forward and surrounds the head of the table.

Presley glares down at Victoria. "Do you *ever* get tired of being a soulless black hole? You're freaking pathetic."

Tanner spreads his hands on the table, and leans in close. "We came here to find you so we could prove to Melanie there's no way you'd cheat on her with Victoria. Instead we find you here wrapped around that empty shell. Are you universally stupid, man?" He straightens and backs away. "You're not the guy I thought you were."

"We were ju—"

Adam chimes in. "What the hell are you doing, Trey?"

Trey looks past the others to me. "Melanie . . ."

Again, he attempts to get up, but Victoria grabs his arm and yanks him back down. Her soggy mascara has run all over the shoulder of his white Hurley T-shirt. He notices the stain, and then his eyes move to Victoria.

"Looks like she's marked her territory," Val says.

Bear works his way to the front of the group, booming, "Victoria!"

She looks up at him, her expression distraught.

"You can consider this the only friendly warning you're likely to get from me," Bear says. "You think you're alpha around here, but you aren't. There's a monster that lives in Melanie. She *will* win. You need to step off now because you're playing with fire."

Trey opens his mouth to speak, but I beat him to it.

"There's no point, Trey! You've made your choice. I have zero interest in playing a game of slap and tickle with Captain Save-a-Hoe."

The guys' mouths drop open. Hiram guffaws.

"You're pathetic," I snarl. "If you wanted Victoria, why didn't you just say so and leave?"

Victoria bows her head over the table. Her back rocks with a gasping torrent of sobs to the point that I almost feel sorry for her. Finley, forever the sweetheart of our group, reaches over the table and sets a hand on her arm. She holds her other hand to Trey. Shoulders slumped, looking dejected, he takes her hand and stands.

To my surprise, Finley slides in and claims the vacated seat next to the sobbing troll.

When I hit Finley with a death glare, she shoots me one of her disappointed-mom looks.

I couldn't care less if Victoria's upset. I don't usually root for the pain of others, but where Victoria is concerned, I'm done.

Trey takes two steps toward me, but I have nothing to say to him.

I pull my backpack around and yank my Discman out of the front pouch. I slip on my headphones and hit the play button. The hostile, hard-hitting sounds of Stone Temple Pilots' "Dead and Bloated" blasts into my ears.

It's exactly the soundtrack I need for the moment I give up on my soulmate.

When Trey follows and catches up to me, I hit him with a look of indifference—a look I've never given him before now. My spine straightens, chest rising, as I turn on my stiletto heels and make my way toward the door.

Through the driving beat of the music, I hear Presley's parting shot to Trey.

"Boy, you were so busy rummaging through that dumpster that you just lost the best thing that ever happened to you."

My heart shattered, I leave Snow White's alone, while keeping an eye out for trouble.

CHAPTER *28*

I look down at my hands and close my eyes. I'm not going to be able to focus on school until I talk to Trey. There's a giant knot in the pit of my stomach, and my chest aches. Add to that my fear of being on my own against the Drones, and I'm a mess. Trey is the only reason I've felt safe.

The girls followed me back to school, while the guys stayed behind to talk to Trey.

Maybe it's better that I stay busy. "We might as well hang the posters," I tell them as we reach our lockers. "We'll get excused absences from first period if we're doing student council stuff, and I don't want you guys getting in trouble for missing class because my boyfriend sucks."

After I trade in my stilettos for a more comfortable pair of All Stars, the girls and I work our way through each of the halls, and by the time we're done, we've covered all the quads, the lunchroom, and the commons in flashy, star-adorned poster boards. We finish just as the bell rings, and all at once we're surrounded by groups of students eager to learn the details.

When the second-period tardy bell rings, we all wave goodbye.

I get to biology class, and the first thing I notice is the empty desk behind mine—where Victoria usually sits. It's a relief, to say the least. After I take my seat, my mind immediately wanders to Trey and what he might be doing. *Maybe I need to be worried about* who *Trey is doing.* I blink back tears as I try to focus on the worksheet in front of me.

Behind me, I hear Victoria's two Drone friends snickering and whispering to each other.

"Maybe Tori should make her move," I hear one of them say. "Looks like Trey's more available than we thought."

My palms break out in a sweaty mess, and my heart feels like it's going to explode. I shrink into my shell, feeling the old, insecure Melanie roar to the surface.

My pager vibrates on my hip, causing me to jump. I discretely press the button, hoping it's Trey. Presley's number flashes across the screen, followed by the number eight. I flip open my notebook and scan the inside cover, where I've written our friends' code list.

An eight means "come outside."

Deciding I can't be here anymore, I throw my stuff back into my pack. When I approach her desk, tears streaming down my face, Ms. Becksworth doesn't ask questions. She silently hands me a hall pass and dismisses me with a sympathetic nod.

The hall outside the classroom is empty.

I make my way down the stairs and out through the double doors of the two-story building. I find Presley by the commons building phone bank with Finley and Valerie. They come to me, hugging me when they see the tears streaming down my face.

"I swear I can feel your heart breaking from across campus," Finley says, gripping my arm. "Come on, chickadee. We're getting out of here."

I must look confused because Valerie says, "We're ditching. I don't want to scare you, but I saw Joel sneaking around with Stan. We need to get you out of here."

We head across campus, eating up the ground quickly with long, purposeful strides. I don't know if this is the best idea, but I don't want to be here, unprotected, if Joel's here. We make a beeline for our rigged gate but stop short when we see two of the school's yellow-jacket-wearing security wannabes patrolling the perimeter.

"Abort mission," Val hisses. "Yellow jackets."

We scamper out of view and hide behind a giant brick pillar.

Presley peeks around the edge and watches for a time. She turns back to us. "Go! Hurry! They aren't looking!"

We rush past the cafeteria and slip into the back alley. We make it around the corner, but find the sliding gate closed and padlocked.

I'm thoroughly frustrated. "Security's tight today, but Joel and his lackey manage to get in? Unreal!" I snarl, "Screw it. We're jumping that wall." I stride with purpose to the giant metal dumpster backed against the wall, hike up my leg, putting my Converse-clad foot into the rail slot, and hoist myself up onto the lid.

"Melanie Slate! I'd know that butt anywhere," a familiar voice calls out.

I freeze on top of the dumpster, which shifts slightly, nearly sending me tumbling. When I recover my balance, I turn carefully and lock eyes with Ms. G. She doesn't appear amused.

Today is not *my day.*

I hop down beside my friends and meet the counselor's confounded gaze.

"What are you doing climbing up there?" Ms. G asks. "You're in a skirt, mooning the entire student body." She crosses her arms and scans our guilty faces. "Who would like to explain?"

We exchange nervous glances, each waiting for another of us to speak up.

Finally, Presley throws up her hands. "All right," she says. "Here it is. Trey's a jackass. He's playing Melanie. It came out last week after he and Melanie started dating, that he was all hot and heavy with Victoria over the summer, which is disgusting enough, but this morning we found him snuggled up to Victoria at Snow White's."

Ms. G does her best to hide her amusement. "Melanie, did you ask Trey why he was with Victoria?"

"Ms. G," Val says, "does it really matter? He had his arm around her. She was practically sitting on his lap."

"Would it help if you and Trey came to my office and talk things out together?"

"Maybe," I say with a shrug. "I don't know."

She unclips the walkie-talkie from her belt and radios to the office. "Main office, this is Ms. G. Please send for Trey Valdez and have him report to me right away." She clicks off and gives me a pointed look. "One way or another, we'll get to the bottom of this."

The bell rings.

"You all head to class," she says to the others. "Melanie will let you know what happens."

"I saw Joel on campus not long before we tried to leave," Val adds hastily.

Ms. G rolls her eyes. "That's impossible, Valerie. He's expelled, and security have an eye out for him."

The girls look dubious but nonetheless decide to trust Ms. G, and Valerie gives her a high five before they hurry off to class.

"All right," Ms. G says, ushering me back toward the Magnet office. "Let's go see what we can find out from Trey. I can sniff out a lie like a springer spaniel hunting a pheasant."

We cut a fast trail across campus and down the stairway to the Magnet office, where Ms. G gestures me into her office. She remains in the waiting area and then closes the door between us.

A moment later, I hear her say, "Trey, it's nice to see you. Please head into my office and have a seat. I'll be right in."

The door opens, and Trey stops short when he sees me sitting on the other side of Ms. G's desk. "Melanie, thank God. We need to talk."

I stare up at him, saying nothing.

Trey deflates and sits in the chair next to me. He glances over with something close to panic in his eyes.

The office door is standing open, and I can see Ms. G sitting in the reception area just out of Trey's line of sight. She gives me a slight nod, and I take a deep breath. Seems Ms. G is giving us some time to work things out on our own, but I know she'll come in if I need help.

I turn to Trey, unsure what to say. He meets my angry glare head-on.

Finally, he sighs. "Full disclosure. Victoria called me last night and told me she needed to talk."

Interesting. Honesty points for him. "You didn't tell *me* you were going to meet with her. I didn't even hear from you yesterday." I'm suddenly enraged and can't seem to keep my voice down. "You didn't tell me you dated her all summer!"

"It's not what—"

"You were draped all over her, Trey!"

"Melanie."

Ms. G's sharp voice from the other room startles me out of my sputtering anger. She steps inside her office and crouches down beside me. "Give Trey a chance to explain." She turns to Trey. "Better make it good. The red flags aren't in your favor."

Trey, beside himself, looks from Ms. G to me. "Okay, one thing at a time. Victoria's been struggling with our sudden breakup. I didn't want to be a jerk, so I agreed to meet her. For the record, I was *not* getting back together with her."

"Were you with Victoria yesterday?"

Trey sighs. "No, Melanie. I admit I needed some downtime. I was doing my own thing, by myself."

"Okay, what did you do?" Ms. G asks.

"I'd be happy to give you that answer," Trey says with an impish grin, "but you're going to have to step out in the hall with me if you want to hear it."

Ms. G's eyes twinkle. She's always up for shenanigans. She follows Trey into the hall. I strain my ears, but can't hear anything. They're gone for only a few moments, and when they return, Ms. G winks at me.

"Anyone want to fill me in?" I ask.

They shake their heads, grinning conspiratorially.

I huff.

"Don't huff," Ms. G says. "It's unbecoming. You'll find out when the time's right." She turns to Trey. "All right, young man. You've still got some questions to answer. Why did you lie about how long you two dated?"

He sighs and rubs his forehead. "Yes, I lied. Victoria and I were more than a fling. We spent the entire summer together. We also went to a couple of the dances together. I've got some history with her. I shouldn't have lied to you about it."

"But *why* did you lie?"

Trey closes his eyes, leans his head back, and crosses his arms over his chest. After a long pause, he says, "My intentions were good, but obviously my execution was bad." He opens his eyes and looks from me to Ms. G. "Look, here it is: Victoria and I were still on and off when Melanie and I met. Being on student council was everything to her. She tried to get me to join, but I don't like Joel and his Drones. They're rude and they're dangerous. The more Victoria hung out with them, the worse she got. My girl slipped through my fingers and became someone I barely knew."

My heart's thudding in my ears, and I'm trying not to cry.

"I'm sorry, Melanie. I know that's hard for you to hear."

I nod, swallowing back the tears. I refuse to cry right now.

"I'm sorry I didn't tell you sooner. And I'm sorry I downplayed my relationship with her. My intentions were good, I promise. But I obviously didn't handle it right."

I look down at my lap. "I told you I was done with the Victoria drama. I meant it."

Trey slumps, looking worried.

I rise from the chair, thank Ms. G, and head for the door.

"Melanie, are we okay?" Trey calls out.

I turn back, but my feelings on the matter are firm. "I'm not going to play games with you, Trey. Or Victoria. I refuse to keep playing *Where's Waldo*, looking for little clues to surface about your tawdry love affair with her. We're a week in and you're already lying to me. I love you, Trey, but I'm out."

I walk out and head to the reception desk for a tardy slip.

CHAPTER *29*

Nearly blind with tears, I turn out of the office and rush down the hall. I make it as far as the stairs, where a hand snakes out from the alcove and grabs my arm. Before I can react, I'm yanked under the stairs. The alcove has a door at the back that opens to a storage closet, and I'm shoved inside.

The door closes behind me with a slam.

Terror shoots up my spine as I attempt to feel my way around in the dark. I trip on something and stumble right, my head striking something metal.

I right myself, but I'm seeing stars.

A flicker of fire from a lighter illuminates Joel's face. He grins maliciously. Behind him, Victoria's usually pretty face looks menacing in the shadow cast by the flame. She narrows her eyes at me and sneers.

I wait for panic to overwhelm me, but it unexpectedly doesn't. Suddenly, I've had enough of this situation. I'm sick of the Drones, I'm beyond sick of Victoria, and as much as Joel terrifies me, I've hit my drama quotient for the week. I sigh and roll my eyes, hitting Joel with an irritated look.

"What the hell is it with you?" I ask him. "You can't get anyone to screw you willingly, so you have to force them?"

"I do it this way because I enjoy it."

I snort, and the last of my terror dissipates on a wave of sarcasm. "You do it because you're a bent-ass, pitiful little boy who needs therapy and a decent mother."

"You leave my mother out of this," he snarls.

"That sorry bitch raised a real piece of work. Quit hunting girls and grow the hell up! Your mother should be ashamed to have raised a son who so obviously isn't decent enough to feel bad about hurting people."

Well, that did it. Joel grabs the front of my shirt with both fists and slams me against the metal supply shelf at my back. It knocks the air out of me. He smiles sadistically and presses his body against mine.

I glance Victoria's way. She's holding the Zippo lighter, and her eyes are huge. When her mouth drops open, I see realization light in her eyes.

She didn't know what he was planning. She never believed the accusations against Joel. Not until now.

She turns, dropping the lighter, and opens the door. Light floods in, and I take a quick look around to get my bearings because I know what's coming. She slips out, making her escape, and lets the door close behind her.

Once again, I'm plunged into darkness with a monster.

When Joel's hand grips my thigh and squeezes hard, something shifts in me. A sense of profound calm slides up my spine. Frantically, I reach behind me for something heavy. My fingers find what feels like a gallon jug on the shelf just above my head. I swing it, connecting with Joel's face. In the pitch black, he never saw it coming.

He screams, falling to the side, and I reach past him, groping blindly for the door.

When my hand finds the knob, I wrench the door open with a shout, and light floods into the tiny closet. Joel squints and grimaces from the floor. Rage surges up from my gut. I reach down and grab Joel by his shirt. Adrenaline blazes through me as I heave him up, slinging him through the door.

I rush after him and stalk to where he's attempting to get up. "I've had *enough*!" I snarl.

Trey, Victoria, and Ms. G run around the corner in time to watch me shove Joel off his feet. He hits the tile and I rear back, gut-kicking him as hard as I can.

He groans.

I kneel, clutch a handful of his hair, and wrench his head back to look me in the eye. "The next time you touch me, I'm going to break you. Consider that a promise." I glance up at Trey and snarl, "Come to watch the show?"

"Victoria came and told us what's happening," he explains. "I planned to drag Joel out and beat him unconscious, but it looks like you didn't need me."

I step away from Joel and turn to meet Victoria's gaze. "Thanks for helping."

She nods, her eyes wide. "I didn't realize," she whispers. "I'm sorry."

Campus security hauls ass around the corner and drags Joel up off the floor.

"You've been expelled," says the shorter of the two. "You shouldn't be here."

Joel wrenches free of the officer and makes a break for the door.

Stunned, I stare at the guards. "Seriously? You're just going to stand there? What does that maniac have to do for you people to act? Go after him!"

"He's gone," the taller guard says. "You're safe."

I show my inner thigh, already purple from a fast-growing bruise. "Oh, yeah. I'm clearly safe."

Trey crosses the distance and kneels to examine the bruise.

"Get up," the shorter guard snaps. "That isn't appropriate."

I glance from Ms. G, to Victoria, to Trey before hitting the security officer with a baffled expression. "Let me get this straight. My boyfriend, or her boyfriend, or whatever he is, looking at a bruise on my thigh left by a known rapist is a problem, but the person that hurt me is free to run away while you stand here like a moron?"

The guards look confused, unsure of what to do.

I turn to Ms. G. "You people need to seriously reevaluate how you handle shit around this place."

As the security officer attempts to scold me for cussing, Ms. G raises a hand to silence him. "She's not wrong." Ms. G turns to me. "I'm calling the police. We need to report this. Let's head back down to my office."

Trey attempts to grab my hand, and I shake him off. I catch up to Ms. G, leaving Trey and Victoria in the hall.

CHAPTER 30

The auditorium lights dim, and the sound of trumpets, like a Renaissance court coronation, ring out over the public address system. The stage lights come on, revealing red columns on either side, a podium in the center, and four risers—one for each grade's homecoming royalty.

The audience erupts in cheers as Arch strides to the podium. "Good morning! I'm Arch Terani, your student body president, and I welcome you to our 1992 homecoming court coronation ceremony!"

More cheers, whoops, and hollers fill the auditorium.

Arch flashes his devastating smile and throws up devil horns. When the crowd quiets, he continues. "I'm here to tell each and every one of you that this year's homecoming dance will be epic," he says. "Your new student council is working hard for *you*!"

More cheers and whistles follow every section of his speech.

Arch is alive with energy, amping up the crowd. "Are you ready?" he says.

The audience cheers, but it's not enough to satisfy Arch.

"I *said*, are you ready?"

The students erupt with a cheer so loud I have to cover my ears. My anxiety soars, and my hands are sweating with fear. This crowd creates the perfect environment to hide lurking trouble.

Arch raises a hand for silence, and the roar dies down.

"I present to you," he says, "the ninth-grade prince and *two* princesses: Marcus Vinsky, Presley Verelle, and Melanie Slate!"

I look to my right, where Rich is holding a camcorder, recording every moment. The three of us flash him a smile as we make our way down the aisle, but mine is forced. This should be the new best day of my life, but instead, my eyes dart from side to side, watching for any sign of Joel and his cronies. A spotlight hits us from the second-story balcony, and the crowd erupts again.

I feel completely vulnerable as every set of eyes lights on us.

We make it to the stage, walk up the stairs, and turn to wave. My friends in the honored first row, reserved for the student council, are on their feet, hugging and cheering—easily the loudest people in the audience. I make eye contact with Trey, and he turns, scanning the crowd for potential trouble. Apparently, even though he and I still have no clue where we stand with each other, he's opting to protect me.

I'm surprised Victoria isn't trolling around with him.

We step onto the ninth-grade riser. The other grade representatives are announced and are received with the same vigor.

This is unreal. I've never seen a crowd this excited!

Arch continues, "Now, here is Hiram Friedman, student council vice president, with bouquets for our princesses and homecoming queen."

Hiram, grinning from ear to ear, steps onto the stage and stands at Arch's side. The student body goes wild. Hiram waves to the crowd and then walks from riser to riser, handing a bouquet to each of the ladies. When he finishes, he steps out of the way to make room for the photographer.

"When the bell rings after lunch today," Arch says into the microphone, "everyone is to report to the football field bleachers for the homecoming parade. That means no fifth- and sixth- period classes today! Welcome to your 1992–1993 school year!"

There's a new wave of thunderous applause, proving that the way to these kids' hearts is to give them a few class periods off.

After the noise dies down, Arch pauses. The anticipation of the crowd grows to the point that students all through the auditorium are leaning forward.

Arch bends slowly to the microphone. "Are you going to be there?" he booms. "Seven tomorrow night. The Roosevelt Hotel ballroom. Is everyone ready to be a star in Hollywood?"

The room explodes, and everyone is on their feet, stomping and screaming. The rumble grows louder and louder, causing the floor to vibrate.

For as long as I live, I will never forget this moment.

—

The east end of the football field looks like an ant hill.

People come and go, busily carrying decorations to their floats. There are more floats than I expected, and for everyone else, the excitement is electric.

Meanwhile, I'm a wreck, searching constantly for any sign of danger.

A guy walks past wearing a white dress shirt and black slacks, and I gasp, grabbing Presley's arm. She alerts Marcus, who rushes to the guy and whips him around. Turns out, it's just someone headed to the choir float.

Marcus gestures to the float. "There's fifty of them, Mel. You need to calm down."

We pass a semi-trailer flatbed where members of the football team are decorating a giant red football helmet perched on the end closest to the cab. The head cheerleader and quarterback are dating, and we overhear that they plan to stand inside the helmet together. The rest of the cheerleaders and players are going to ride on the float and throw T-shirts into the bleachers. It's a good thing they have such a big vehicle because there must be 130 of them. They're all excitedly taping red and black fringe to the edge of the bed of the truck and giant stars to the sides of the enormous helmet. They look like they're having fun, all sporting their football jerseys and cheerleading uniforms.

The media club float is my favorite that we pass. They put a giant television set on the back of their small flatbed truck with "*Do you want your Htv?*" scrawled in huge letters, a clever play on the Mtv commercials.

After a contemplative breath, I turn to Presley and Marcus. "My intuition's nagging at me."

They stop, concerned, and Adam walks over to join us as I say, "At this point I'm worried that Joel's going to try to kill me."

I look across the way at our friends on our student council float and spot Trey and Victoria. My mouth drops open, and I gesture to them. "You have to be kidding."

"If it helps," Adam says, "she seems to be following him around. He's rather irritable about it, actually." He grins, seeming thrilled by Trey's conundrum.

Trey walks over with Victoria at his heels. She's like a lost puppy. When he gets to us, he rolls his eyes and turns to hit Victoria with a look of annoyance. "Seriously, Tori. Please stop. I need to talk to Melanie."

"I'd like to speak with Melanie also," she says quietly.

"You'll both have to wait," Adam says. "Melanie's intuition is firing up."

Arch, Bear, Tanner, and Darren hop off the student council float and come our way just in time to hear this, and all turn to me, curious.

"My intuition's been nagging at me," I explain. "But I can't figure it out. It's too vague. It's making me a nervous wreck."

Trey turns a worried look my way, and I turn a cold shoulder on him and Victoria both.

Unfortunately, this puts me directly facing Adam, who's staring at me with penetrating eyes. He puts an arm around me. He doesn't say anything, but he looks worried. He squeezes me hard, while looking around for trouble. Trading one ex-boyfriend for another is annoying, but I can't help my amusement as I glance back and see the pained expression on Trey's face.

"No doubts about her intuition, huh?" Arch asks Adam.

Adam shakes his head. "I believe her. It's proven itself."

"We only have an hour to put the finishing touches on the float." Arch glances at the guys. "We need to keep an eye out. I don't want Melanie, Presley, or Marcus worried about this today."

Trey must give the others a look behind my back because everyone but him and Victoria make a hasty retreat.

That's just great.

I roll my eyes, and Trey nervously cracks his neck. Victoria huffs, silently fuming. The tension lasts for longer than I can stand, and I start to walk away.

Trey grabs my arm. "I'm going to help with whatever's coming."

I roll my eyes and sarcastically say, "Hurray!"

He looks exasperated but nonetheless holds out his hand. "Send me what you've got."

I sigh. "Fine."

I take his hand, and the energy wraps and melds like it always does with us. Our eyes meet and Trey smirks.

"We've still got it, Melanie."

I roll my eyes and look away, unfortunately catching Victoria's confused gaze. She looks down at our clasped hands before hitting Trey with a puzzled look.

Trey studies the pulse. "Feels like nighttime, but you're right. It's vague."

When he drops my hand, Victoria turns to me.

"In Trey's defense, I've tried every trick in my arsenal, and he wants nothing to do with me. He's only interested in you. I'm really sorry for the whole Joel thing—the closet. I had the situation all wrong."

I cross my arms and huff. But after some thought, I relent. "I don't appreciate you stirring up shit for me every chance you've had since the first day of school."

Victoria nods, admitting, "I was out of line. Honestly, I saw you as competition." She nods to Trey. "Clearly I was right about that."

I raise an eyebrow. "You hit on Adam in front of Trey and half the school. You cannonballed you and Trey all on your own."

Victoria scrunches up her face. "Good point."

I give her a skeptical look, and she returns it. After a moment we both smile the slightest bit and look away.

"If we ever become friends," Victoria says, "we could run this place."

I chuckle and raise an eyebrow her way. "If we ever become friends, Hell might freeze over."

She grins back. "Think we could settle on neutral hatred with a side of catty amusement?"

"Deal."

We shake hands and walk together to the student council float, leaving behind a bewildered Trey.

Bear hops down off the truck bed. "I'm going to check on the float progress for all the clubs and teams. I need to make sure the yearbook photography team are getting pictures. It'll make a great story in the yearbook *and* the school paper."

"Good idea, Bear," Arch says. "Looks like I picked the right guy for that student council job! Do you need help?"

"Actually, yes. Hey, Chad, can you come with me? You know more of the Regulars than I do, and it'll be a good way for us to show our new comingled school cooperation."

Chad hops down and fist-bumps Bear. "I've got your back. Let's do this." He tosses a roll of red streamers to Tanner.

The two hurry off, and Tanner gets to work draping streamers on each of the fifteen directors' chairs on our float. Going with the "Everyone's a Star in Hollywood" theme, we thought the chairs would be a fun way to tie in that we're the student council directing everything behind the scenes. Our float is covered in giant shiny red and gold stars, and Hiram's Hollywood sign for the photo backdrop is tied to the back of the truck cab.

"Marcus, Melanie, and Presley!" Darren calls out. "You need to go meet the driver for your homecoming court convertible. He's a nice guy, and the car is sweet—a red 1957 Ford Thunderbird. The rest of us already met the owner, and drooled all over the car. The top will be down, so you can sit along the back."

We make our way toward the cherry-red dream car. Trey comes along, watching for trouble. At least Victoria doesn't follow us. Presley and Marcus hold hands, gazing at each other, and I sigh as an awkward silence stretches between me and Trey.

The homecoming parade was everything we expected it to be. The theater department won the float competition—no big surprise considering the set-and-prop warehouse they get to pull from. Their float featured a perfectly painted giant backdrop with all the classic Hollywood landmarks, like the Capitol Records Building and the Hollywood Bowl. A group of theater students strutted around the float, dressed as James Dean, Elvis Presley, Madonna, Michael Jackson, and Marilyn Monroe, who stood on a raised platform with a fan blowing up her white skirt. Not even Arch's enthusiasm could compete with the thrill of Marilyn's skirt wafting above her waist. She wore red shorts under her skirt, but the student body's imagination clearly won out.

True to his word, Arch announced the ninth-grade court just as our cherry-red ride pulled up center stage in the middle of the field. As Marcus, Presley, and I hopped off the student council float and climbed into the back of the T-Bird, the excited crowd roared.

Arch had thought of everything. Dance tickets were raffled off to ten lucky winners, and at the end of the pep rally, a mass of red and black confetti was released over the football field and bleachers. Everyone was so excited by the time the rally came to a close, they could hardly wait for the big dance the next evening. We all stayed for the football game, and Hollywood High beat Fairfax in a landslide.

All in all, the day was a huge success, and we got through it with no big issues.

Sadly, I was such a mess I was barely able to enjoy any of it. At least Victoria seemed placated by our almost-reconciliation.

CHAPTER 31

When we hit Robertson and Pico, I'm completely turned around. I've never been to this area of Beverly Hills, but Val, who has been to Hiram and Arch's house before, seems to know where she's going.

Now that Trey and I are on the outs, I got ready for the party and rode with the girls. I need a girls' night, but I'm dreading that we're all staying at Arch and Hiram's. An awkward sleepover with Trey isn't high on my list of good times.

Val takes a left onto a side street, and it's obvious from half a block away that we're in the right place when I spot a three-story house on the left boiling over with kids like a swarming beehive. There are teenagers everywhere—along the sidewalk, covering the front lawn, and lining the long staircase to the third-story balcony.

We park and Val turns to us. "Here we go!" She glances my way and grins. "Hiram and Arch's parties are legendary. Get ready for the best night of your life."

I can't seem to muster their enthusiasm. I'm too much of a wreck.

We climb out of the car, straighten our outfits, and walk toward the chaos. We've all dressed in black, and my skintight bustier top and bouncy goth-inspired tutu skirt even earns a compliment from hard-to-impress Presley. Everyone we pass turns a head, their conversations dying as they stop and stare. When a couple of wolf whistles pierce the air in our wake, I can't help but grin.

Suddenly, mercifully, I feel excitement bubbling up. *This might be a good time, after all.*

We head up the stairs past a long row of teens lounging against the railing, then turn onto the spacious balcony.

"What's up, *party people!*" blares through the open door as a voice riles up the crowd over a microphone. A wall of sound greets us as we enter the living room, where a deejay is set up at the far side of the room. No regular old stereo system for this gathering.

I've entered a whole new stratosphere of cool.

When Trey sees me, his mouth drops open.

Shamelessly, I toss my curled chestnut hair over my shoulder.

Trey pushes away from the wall, leaving his conversation with Chad and Kelsey, and makes his way to me.

"You were great today at the coronation," he says.

He's obviously still interested, and I melt a little. I smile the tinniest bit, flirtatiously looking up at him through my lashes.

Victoria chooses that moment to sidle up beside Trey.

Who invited her?

My face falls and hit I Trey with cold eyes before walking off.

He sighs and returns to Chad and Kelsey—with Victoria following.

A group of partiers form a cypher circle in the middle of the room. A guy named Demitri is the first to slide into the middle. He quickly proves why he's the best dancer at the school. He hits a top rock, his muscled body drops into a perfect back bend, and then he springs up into a full aerial split.

Javier jumps in, squaring off against Demitri, and pulls off a flawless quadruple turn into a wild double leg fan-kick leap. Javier is Demitri's best friend and easily rivals Demitri on the dance floor.

The crowd goes wild, cheering and dancing around them. I can't help but openly admire Javier. Dark and handsome is my type, after all, and Javier's got both in spades. I glance Trey's way. He's clearly irritated. When I smirk, he rolls his eyes.

Arch, carrying two beer bottles in each hand, elbows through the crowd and makes his way to us. "Ladies, so glad you could make it," he shouts over the blaring of "More and More" by Captain Hollywood Project.

He hands us each a beer. "Make yourselves at home. The Burners are toking up in the backyard. The Losers we don't want here are milling about in the front yard. And the rest of our group is in the kitchen, making margaritas. Oh, and Bear's in Hiram's room with Darren. Pick your poison." Arch grins and slips back into the crowd, making his way with surprising grace, given his wide shoulders.

"What'll it be, gals?" Val asks, raising an eyebrow. "Burners, Losers, Bear's witchy crowd, or Margaritaville?"

"Margaritaville."

Finley makes the call, and we weave through the partygoers toward the kitchen.

Just as we enter, Hiram pushes the button on the blender, and green margarita mix flies in every direction, splattering the ceiling, cabinets, and nearly every person in the vicinity.

Apparently, this isn't the first time this has happened because Presley had the foresight to yell, "Duck!" as we came through the doorway. We managed to hunker down and avoid getting coated by the mess.

"Forgot to take the spoon out of the blender again, boys?" Presley says as we rise from behind the island. "You know, there's a lid up there." Eyes dancing with good humor, she points to the cabinet above the sink.

Bear walks in, taking a look around. "What the . . ."

"Hey, help me clean up this mess!" Hiram yells to no one in particular.

We each grab a handful of towels from a drawer next to the dishwasher and start mopping up the disaster. The whole room smells like a tequila-infused sauna.

"Kenji, grab that lid," Hiram orders, pointing at the cabinet shelf that's just out of his reach.

Kenji snags the blender lid without even having to stretch. Being tall has its perks.

The margaritas are swiftly remade, and red solo cups are filled to the brim with the slushy mix. I'm still holding the beer Arch gave me. I don't know how people can drink this stuff. I need to discard it without being rude. Trey swoops in and solves my problem, taking the beer and replacing it with a margarita.

I wish he would just let me enjoy the night without getting all up on me.

My thoughts are interrupted as Adam strides aggressively into the kitchen.

"He's here," Adam says.

His tone is the deadliest I've ever heard from a teenage boy, and my intuition blazes to life.

"Melanie?" Trey says.

My chest seizes. The pain is so bad I can't speak. I grip Trey's hand and send a pulse.

His eyes widen. "This is about to be bad. Joel's not alone."

"Exactly right," Adam says.

"This is what I've been waiting for," I manage to choke out.

Trey releases my hand and fills in the rest of the group, who can't read my premonition.

Bear looks less concerned than the other guys. Not surprising because he's twice Joel's size. "I'll keep an eye on you, Mel," he says, "but stay out of the way and let us handle this."

I snort. *Highly unlikely.*

We file out of the kitchen, with me at the back of the line, and move across the living room. Finley, Val, Presley, and I huddle against the wall while the guys line up shoulder to shoulder in the center of the room. At the last moment, Val steps into line next to Chad. No one objects; she's tough as nails and looking to settle a score. I step up beside her, and we exchange a look, partners in the bizarre sisterhood created by Joel's rape attempts.

Joel struts through the door, followed by nine of his Drones, each a carbon copy of the other in their black slacks, white button-downs, and black ties hanging loose around their necks. They line up opposite us, looking menacing.

The music stutters to a halt, and the deejay backs into the dining room.

Tension fills the air. It's so thick, I can barely breathe. Our guys clearly have them with size, but they're outnumbered. As long as no one pulls a weapon, we have a shot. Adam inhales to speak, but before he can get a word out, Trey steps forward.

Panic rises. *What is hell is he doing?*

Trey rushes Joel, grabs him by the front of the shirt, heaves him up, and throws him through the living room window.

Joel lands on the balcony with a thud.

There's a moment of deafening silence punctuated only by the tinkle of falling glass, and then. . .

All hell breaks loose as Joel's crew lunge toward my friends. Fists start flying. The sound is terrifying. People are screaming and running for cover, clearing room for the brawl.

Arch hits a Drone with an uppercut that lays him flat. He isn't moving.

I frantically turn my head and watch as Bear backs a pair of Drones into a corner. The two cower, realizing they're outgunned by sheer size. Bear holds them there with an evil look. Kenji takes over, promising Bear he'll knock the guys out if they dare to move. Though a harmless pacifist, Kenji is almost as mountainous as Bear, so the guys pinned in the corner aren't likely to cross him.

Hiram takes a wicked punch to the cheek. He straightens, shaking his head like he's trying to clear the ringing in his ears. Bear turns and grabs his attacker by the collar and tosses him into a wall.

I'm briefly frozen in place when Val races across the room and leaps onto the back of the biggest Drone. She grabs him by the neck and tugs him backward just as he goes to sucker-punch Marcus in the back. The violence is getting out of hand, and it's moving closer to me.

I have to find a way out of this corner!

Presley, covering Finley, races along the edge of the room toward the front door. She looks my way and shouts, *"Mel! Move!"*

I slide out of the way just in time to avoid getting plowed into by a thug Adam tackles into the wall just inches away.

Adam spares a moment to look my way. "Run, Mel!"

I turn my head to the sound of someone roaring and see Stan racing toward me. I jazz-split down through his legs and shoulder roll to avoid him. Demitri picks me up, getting me in a waist tuck. I grab his arms, leaning against his chest for leverage as I lash out with a fan kick that catches Stan unaware. My stiletto heel smacks him at full force in the face, leaving a long, deep gouge in his cheek. When Stan drops to the floor in pain, Demitri sets me down, flashing a heart-stopping grin at me.

God, he's gorgeous. I rattle my head, trying to focus on the brawl around me.

Amused, Demitri says, "Nice to see you, Mel. Good times, huh?"

Unfortunately, I don't have time to flirt with Demitri because Stan has backup.

I turn and catch a Drone fist to my gut. It sends me tumbling backward, ass over teakettle, through the broken window. I land on my knees next to Joel and Trey, who are fist fighting on the balcony.

Before anyone can do anything, Stan launches himself through the door.

I jump to my feet to counter his advance, but he's too fast and shoves me back hard, screaming, "Time to pay up, bitch!"

I fly toward the railing, seeing Trey's terrified eyes as my back catches the balcony's edge and I flip over.

I hear my name being screamed by my friends above. Out of nowhere, a hand grabs me. All at once, I'm dangling by one arm from the third story, and I'm so scared I can't even scream. Joel looks down at me with the most terrified expression I've ever seen.

"Melanie!" he screams. "Hold on!"

Of all people, Joel's the one who saved me from plunging three stories. The last thing I want is my life in his hands. My terror-bent mind rattles. Joel has it out for me, so why does he seem like he cares whether I live or die?

An icy thought seizes me. *If he lets me die, he can't torture and rape me!*

I hear Stan scream, "DROP HER! END THIS!"

Joel's expression morphs, pushing past the point of sanity—if he ever had any to begin with. I'm about to die, and the last thing I'm going to see is the contorted Jekyll-and-Hyde face of this lunatic.

The world goes eerily quiet.

Then, I see a pair of hands wrap around Joel's shoulders while I hear a fresh fight blaze to life on the balcony. It has to be Bear trying to pull Joel back while someone else deals with Stan. Bear's the only one on the balcony with the sheer size to pull him backward with my weight hanging from Joel's hand. He hefts him back, but not enough.

"Kenji, help!" Bear screams.

For me, time slows. There's no way Bear will get me over the railing before Joel lets go.

Joel's grip loosens around my wrist, and my body and brain go numb.

Only a few seconds have passed, but it feels like an eternity.

Suddenly Trey is leaning over the railing, grabbing for my hand just as Joel lets go.

Trey strains, trying to hold on. He turns red, face contorted, and then with sheer brute strength, he pulls. He gets my hand as high as the railing while Arch leans over the edge, grabbing me under the arms. The two of them haul me up to the safety of the balcony.

Bear turns in a rush and hits Joel so hard that there's a sound of bones cracking. Joel drops, out cold.

A pair of arms wraps around me. It's Trey, and he's guiding me away from the railing. I'm shaking so hard my teeth are chattering, and my legs barely work. My hearing is distorted from the sound of my heartbeat in my ears. My eyes won't focus.

"She's in shock," I think I hear someone say.

Trey tips my head back, and our eyes meet. I can feel through our connection how traumatized he is from nearly losing me.

My legs go out from under me, and Trey gently lowers me to the floor of the balcony.

"Melanie, you're in shock," he says. "I need you to look at me. Breathe in . . . out . . . in . . . out."

His voice is so far away. My head lolls to the side.

I gaze into his eyes.

Trey is leaning over me, and all at once, I'm *decided* about us. . . I kiss him with the kind of passion he's tried to slow down between us.

My right hand snakes weakly around the back of his neck. He loses his balance and falls, landing on top of me. The kiss turns into something laced with fire as he crushes his lips against mine, responding to the tornado of energy swirling around us. We roll across the balcony, and he crushes my shoulder against the wall railing.

All the fear, adrenaline, and shock races from my body on a bolt of energy that burns straight through Trey. His back convulses, his eyes wide. This energetic exchange is twice as intense as the one at the laser show. It's like something new has blasted open in my metaphysical side, something that's going to affect my connection with Trey forever.

I faint dead away.

CHAPTER *32*

Pain.

Hand. Shoulder.

Voices surround me, but they sound far away. They get closer as the pain intensifies. I open my eyes but can't focus, seeing nothing but blurry outlines.

So tired!

Then it all comes rushing back. I remember I'm at Arch and Hiram's. There was a fight, and Trey rescued me—saved me from plummeting off from the balcony.

A moan escapes my mouth as I try again to open my eyes. *Focus, Mel. Blink. Almost there. You can do this. You need to know what's happening.*

A thousand confusing noises all mix together, overwhelming my senses.

"Guys," Presley calls out. "She's waking up."

The sound of footsteps coming closer.

Adam, Darren, Arch, Hiram, and Kenji round the back end of the ambulance and approach the gurney. They're worried. To my right, Bear is holding my hand. I sense he's been there the whole time, like a nurse watching and waiting until his patient wakes up.

"Well, Kitten Little, you sure don't listen real well," he says. "I told to you stay out of the way and we'd handle it." His big bear laugh booms as ambulance lights flash.

Everyone exhales and chuckles softly.

I turn my head, sending fire shooting through my shoulder as my eyes meet Trey's. He laces his fingers with my free hand and pulses a relieved emotion bubble my way. I close my eyes, and his energy starts to revive me.

"Can someone fill me in on what's happened since I decided to take a nap?" I ask.

Arch appears at the end of the gurney. "Joel's Drones scattered and bolted after Bear knocked Joel out. They're torn up pretty bad. We called the cops, and Joel was arrested for attempted murder. He's eighteen, so he'll likely face prison time. They had to take him to the hospital first, though. Trey apparently broke several of Joel's ribs and might have ruptured his spleen."

Trey grimaces sheepishly. "I couldn't take a chance after your premonition. I had to stop him. Joel belongs in jail, and it sounds like that's where he's headed."

I scan the crowd, checking over each of my friends. "Are any of *us* going to jail for assault?"

"Not so far," Hiram says pensively. "But we don't know yet. The Drones are all well connected, and we're worried about their parents pressing charges. Marcus has already called his dad, and he's on his way to take our statements in case any of us need lawyers."

"Is anyone hurt?" I ask.

"Not too bad. A few cuts and bruises. Val has a busted lip, but she kicked ass."

Val throws devil horns in the air, and I smile.

"I think we've all had enough excitement for one night," Presley says. "Mel, I'm glad you're okay. You scared the crap out of us. We couldn't get you to wake up, but Bear and Trey were sure you just needed to rest until the shock wore off. The police want to talk to you."

I groan. "We have to be at the Roosevelt first thing tomorrow morning to set up for the dance."

"We'll worry about that later," Trey says.

A police officer walks up and asks, "Melanie Slate?" When I nod, he continues, "I'd like to confirm that Joel Stamp attempted to drop you from that balcony."

I send a pulse to Trey that I'm conflicted because Joel seemed concerned about trying to save me—at least when I first went over the edge. Trey shakes his head slightly and sends back a pulse that Joel needs to land in jail, and attempted murder is a good way to lock him up so he can't hurt anyone else.

I nod to the officer. "Yes, sir."

The officer thanks me and heads off to handle the other witness interviews. A paramedic steps up and checks my vitals, then looks in my eyes with a flashlight, making me wince. After a moment, he helps me to sitting and gently rotates my shoulder. "You may have torn ligaments. Your shoulder will need to be checked. We can take you to the hospital."

Trey shakes his head. "I don't want her going to any hospital. Joel might be there. I can take her to the urgent care on Fairfax."

The paramedic seems satisfied with that solution.

Slowly, I stand up, a little unsteady on my feet.

The girls grab our overnight bags from Valerie's car, and Valerie calls out, "Mel, I've got your bag. I'll take it upstairs."

I nod my appreciation and watch as the girls head up the staircase to the balcony, with Hiram and some others of the group in tow.

Victoria chooses that moment to walk over and say, "I'm headed out, T."

Trey nods her way and asks, "Are you hurt?"

She shakes her head and crosses to a little blue sedan. She gets in and drives away.

I roll my eyes and huff. As childish as it is, I have to clear up the Victoria mess if this is going to work between us. "Bear, Darren, Tanner," I call out.

They turn and head our way. I sit on the front lawn, my legs still a little wobbly. They take a seat with me, and Trey sits behind me, pulling my back against his chest.

I glare up at him over my shoulder and explain, "I'm sick and freaking tired of dealing with Victoria." I look to the guys, adding, "If Trey and I have a shot at working, then we need to fix this now."

"Can't you lighten up about Victoria now that the two of you had your sort-of truce during the parade prep?" Trey counters.

I lean to the side and hit him with a dazzlingly sarcastic grin, my eyes flashing. "Not until you and I come to an understanding. As much as I know you on a soulmate level, we're still getting to know each other in this lifetime. Welcome to Melanie, where grudges die hard and snark lives forever."

Trey scoffs, amused. "I see. Noted." He raises an eyebrow. "You're bat-shit crazy and somehow it makes you even more appealing."

The guys laugh.

"I need clear boundaries," I say. "And after we return from urgent care, I plan to enjoy the rest of my night." I give Bear and Darren a pointed look. "How about you two Zen masters regulate this mess? I'm still feeling froggy, and Trey's clearly clueless."

Darren breaks into an amused smile.

"All right," Bear says. "Melanie, please calmly summarize how you're feeling."

Damn. Bear's going to be Bear about this. I roll my eyes. "Okay. Here goes nothing."

Trey chuckles. "Don't you mean, 'Here goes everything?'"

I groan, and Bear laughs.

"Give her a minute, Trey," he says. "The two of you don't handle conflict the same way. Your fuse burns out, and you snap back to human. When Melanie's fuse lights, it has to explode before she comes back to herself."

Before I can stop it, a harsh giggle escapes my lips.

Bear turns a hard gaze back to me. "Don't be bitchy. I get that your biting wit is your defense mechanism, but it's not productive right now."

I huff once, hard and fast, and glare at him.

"You asked me to regulate this mess," he says. "You didn't think I'd let you run wild like a tantrum-fueled toddler while I gag Trey's smart mouth, did you?"

"I was kind of hoping," I say.

The guys chuckle, and Trey snorts.

"Fat chance, Kitten Little. All right. Hit us with it."

I suddenly know exactly how I feel, and tears rush to the surface.

"Whatever you're thinking is definitely right," Bear says. "Out with it."

It takes me a moment to pull it together. Finally, I draw a shaky breath and lock eyes with Bear. "Trey's consideration of Victoria over me makes me feel like a ghost again. I'm not going to be a ghost, even for him."

Everyone stops moving, letting my words sink in. They all know how hard I've worked to not be invisible, and they're more than conscious of how I felt as a ghost all those years.

Trey is statue still, not even breathing. He slides sad eyes my way before turning his head slowly to look at Bear. "That's the last thing I want to do," he says.

I swallow a lump in my throat and fight my desire to clam up. I need to get this out to move forward. "I'm sick to death of Trey continuing to be so considerate of Victoria after all the drama she's caused." I look to Trey. "You're always tiptoeing around her, refusing to tell her how it is. It's her or me. Cut-and-dried."

"That's only because you can handle things," Trey says. "You're one of the strongest people I know. Victoria *can't* handle anything. She's not like you. Most people aren't." His expression is earnest, begging me to understand.

He just said the wrong thing.

Suddenly I'm red-hot pissed. "I can handle it? Are you insane? Most of the time I'm a nervous wreck. Until a few weeks ago, I could barely function. Adam taught me to ground and center, which has helped a lot, but I'm not some Viking warrior queen. I need you to understand that."

"It's true," Tanner says. "She's changed *a lot* since the start of the school year."

Bear holds up both hands, and Trey and I look at him.

"Let me try," he says, turning to Trey. "Can Melanie handle it? Of course, she can. She's an Aries, and going into battle is what she does. Melanie will step up every damn time, put on her armor, and kick ass because that's at the core of her being. The bigger question you need to consider is should she have to, and should *you* be the one to make her do that?"

Trey opens his mouth to retort, but Bear, shaking his head,

shuts him down. "I'm not done. You're wrong about this, and I'd appreciate the opportunity to explain why."

Trey's eyes narrow, but he snaps his mouth closed, willing to hear Bear out.

"What I need to get through to you is that *you* feel you owe Victoria kindness. But, in giving her that kindness, you're requiring Melanie to sacrifice her own graciousness. Victoria hasn't earned that from Melanie, and Melanie's grace isn't a gift you get to give."

To his credit, Trey doesn't speak, and instead lets Bear's words sink in.

"I don't blame Melanie for disliking Victoria," Darren says. "She's been a consistent pain in Melanie's ass since the first day of school."

Trey closes his eyes and exhales. "I broke Victoria when I left her," he says. "My leaving has little to do with Melanie in the sense that I was over Victoria's foul attitude already. But it has a lot to do with Melanie in the timing arena. The reason Victoria is so nasty is because she's so insecure. It's a façade. I can tell you firsthand that the pushback Melanie gives her is Victoria's worst social nightmare."

I'm getting pissed again. "Victoria this and Victoria that!" I look at Bear, motioning to Trey. "There's no hope for this guy!"

Bear chuckles. "Melanie, if you were thinking with your head instead of your heart, you'd be taking notes right now. *The Art of War*, Kitten Little. When a warrior is presented facts about their enemy, they should take heed."

"Where you've got it wrong is that I have zero interest in a battle with that hot mess express," I insist. "She's a runaway freight train, but I get to choose whether or not I stand on the tracks. She isn't worth the effort, Bear. At least not for me." The last part is directed at Trey, and I hit him with flashing eyes to punctuate the point.

"I try to be considerate of Victoria because it just makes things easier with her," Trey continues. "I learned when we were dating to anticipate her fits and disarm the bomb before it explodes."

Bear scoffs. "That's where you're going wrong, young Jedi. Choosing Victoria over Melanie is precisely the problem. And again we've come full circle."

"What do you want me to do then?" Trey growls.

Tanner clears his throat. "It's simple."

We all blink in surprise at Tanner's directness.

He takes a deep breath and explains, "I appreciate that you're so aware of Victoria's quirks, Trey. But if you want Melanie, then you have to be with Melanie. You work around Victoria's outbursts because it's easier for you, but Victoria's a nasty freak, and you made a choice to leave her. All you're doing is enabling her and shooting yourself in the foot in the process."

Tanner is the last guy I expected that from. I give him an appreciative look.

"So, Trey," Bear says. "It's the moment of reckoning. This all boils down to a simple question: Is it Victoria or Melanie?"

Trey doesn't miss a beat. "Melanie. That's not even a question."

"Then prove it," Darren says. "Actions speak louder than words, and your actions lately lean toward Victoria."

"I'm sorry. I don't want to lose you over this." Trey looks at me intently. "I get what you're saying, and I'm sorry."

Trey takes my hand and sends a pulse. I've figured out that we can't lie mind to mind, and his message is full of love for me and wanting me back. He sends a second pulse of him being thoroughly finished with Victoria.

"You two get whatever spot you choose to sleep tonight," Bear says. "Tell me where, and I'll get blankets and pillows set up while you're at urgent care."

"The balcony," Trey says. "I want to be alone so we can deal with things."

My usual post-battle hysteria bubbles up, and I raise a seductive eyebrow Trey's way. Not expecting my quick change of mood, Trey throws back his head and laughs.

Bear, Darren, and Tanner grin, and we all get up.

"One balcony love nest, coming right up," Tanner quips.

The three guys head upstairs, while Trey and I walk to his car. He opens my door, and I slide into the passenger seat. The warm silence and smell of his car envelope me. *His car always smells like home*. I draw a deep breath, lean back, and close my eyes, listening as Trey climbs in beside me and closes the driver's side door.

When I open my eyes, Trey's head is in his hands against the steering wheel.

"We made it through your Joel intuition," he says. "It's over."

Alone and finally safe, I whimper as tears roll down my cheeks. The terror of dealing with Joel, and it being over, has pushed me over the edge. Trey takes my hand, and I send a pulse his way of what's wrong with me.

"Baby, you're okay," Trey says. "Come here."

I climb over the center console and sag in his lap with my back against his door. He puts his arms around me and waits patiently until the tears subside.

When I'm calm, he says, "You never fall apart like that."

"Wrong," I say, shaking my head. "I only fall apart with you."

He kisses my forehead and smiles down at me. "This side of you is really endearing."

I rub my face against his chest like a needy toddler, and he hugs me tighter for a second.

When I'm emotionally collected again, I climb back into my seat.

Trey starts the car, and a radio station deejay's enthusiastic voice booms through the speakers. "And now for a song I think we all could use right now."

I smile as the first few notes thrum through the speakers.

"Well, Little Miss Intuitive," Trey says, "what does this song tell you?"

I meet his gaze. "That we're good."

Trey grins at me, and we take off into the night with Bon Jovi's "Keep The Faith" blasting.

CHAPTER 33

Lucky for me, Trey knew the urgent care doctor. Apparently, the guy had treated a number of injured bodyguards that used to work for Trey's dad, and he scooted me in as soon as we arrived. After much fussing and several x-rays, I was released with a shoulder sling. No torn ligaments, but I was instructed to avoid using the arm for a few weeks.

We get back in a little over an hour, and I follow Trey up the long three-story staircase at Hiram and Arch's house. I can't help but laugh when we get to the balcony. Pillows and blankets have been set up on an air mattress. Our jackass friends have cut out ridiculously giant red and pink hearts that they've written less than appropriate things on in black marker. They've taped them up all along the balcony half wall and the wall by the now boarded-up window.

Trey reads a few of them and cracks up. He turns to me and says, "I guess we're back together, in the tackiest possible way." He points to one of the X-rated valentines and reads, "Bow-chicka-boing-boing," and we both crack up.

He grabs my overnight bag, sitting by our makeshift bed, and hands it to me. I head inside to get changed out of my party clothes.

Trey follows me in, and Tanner, who's snuggled up with Finley on the couch, gestures in the direction of the balcony while singing the theme song to *The Love Boat*. We both belt with surprised laughter along with everyone else in the living room.

I head into Hiram's room to change into sweatpants and a tank top. I throw on a hoodie, in case it gets cold, and come back out with my duffel bag.

Trey, leaning against the wall, wearing gym shorts and a tank top, is chatting with the guys. He turns my way and hushes Tanner, who's disappointed by my less than provocative attire.

"Believe me, Tanner," Trey says, "what she's wearing is the best possible choice."

Tanner looks confused. "I don't get it. You have a whole night to yourselves."

I roll my eyes. "This is Trey pumping the brakes."

"You're dead inside if you don't take advantage of tonight," Adam says to Trey.

Trey looks at me and says, "Just taking our time. I'm not screwing this up."

Finley visibly melts. "That is the sweetest thing, ever."

Presley rolls her eyes. She gestures to me, while saying to Trey, "Mel's a rattlesnake, and she gets bored easily. You sure about this plan?"

I shoot her an exasperated look, but Trey just laughs.

"Yes, Pres. I'm sure." He turns to me. "Come on, love. Let's fix what's broken between us. We need time together and sleep. It's been a rough night."

Trey drapes his arm over my shoulder, and we head outside.

We drop our duffel bags, and Trey heads back to the door, cracking it and sliding his hand in to turn out the porch light.

We hear catcalls as he closes the door.

He crosses to me under the soft glow of the full moon, tips up my chin, and says, "My rule still stands. I'm not doing anything with you for the first time on Hiram and Arch's balcony, surrounded by X-rated messages."

I nod. "Understood." I gesture to the suggestive décor and jokingly add, "But, honey. . . It's so romantic."

Trey raises an eyebrow and reads the heart message closest to us. "If the balcony's a rockin' don't come a knockin'."

"I mean, this is really special," I joke.

Trey laughs and shakes his head. Finally, he gestures to the blow-up mattress and says, "After you."

A touch perplexed, I say, "This is supposed to be weird . . . I mean, it *is* weird." I look around at the bizarre balcony setup. "But it's also *not* weird. Is that weird?"

He chuckles and hugs me. "Somehow, no. It's not weird falling asleep next to you. It makes sense—our soulmate connection, and all. What's going to be weird is *not* falling asleep with you on every other night."

"Wonderful. Another thing to keep us up at night."

"Honestly, I think our biggest problem is likely how this bond is becoming so strong, so fast. It's going to far outrun our ages, and I'm already sure the strain of it is going to be taxing."

I raise an eyebrow. "Looks like I'm not the only one with intuition."

I lower myself to our makeshift bed and slide my feet under the covers. The mattress squeaks and squawks its plastic protest. Trey sits, and we do our best to settle in together, cracking up as the mattress continues to serenade us. He props himself up on an elbow, and we laugh again when the mattress squeals.

He plops flat on his back, saying, "Yeah. We're definitely not regaling anyone inside with this thing."

I dissolve in a torrent of giggles and rest my head on Trey's chest. He slides his arms around me, and I have to work a bit to find a position that doesn't disturb my injured shoulder.

"All I wanted was to have you back," Trey says. "I hated fighting with you, and I was worried it was over."

"Can we just be okay?" I ask. "No more fighting?"

He exhales, relieved. He laces his hand with mine and sends a pulse that he loves me. I send a matching pulse back to him, and we both drift off to sleep.

CHAPTER 34

The last zipper is zipped, and our room at the Roosevelt smells like hairspray and perfume. The girls look like rock stars.

Valerie's black dress is skintight with sequins all over the strapless top and a slit up to her hip. No amount of makeup will cover her split lip, but she's decided to shrug it off. Presley's short black leather dress, with its decorative buckles running up the front, is completed by a pair of black leather ankle heels. Finley's in a gorgeous red ruffled dress with a fluffy ruffled skirt, along with a red fascinator hat with a red-and-black feather plume. My short, fitted, black sequined dress has a puffy red-and-black tulle bustle, and I'm wearing red strappy heels.

I've ditched the shoulder sling, just for the night.

Mom pulls a box out of a cooler tucked between the wall and the bed. We gather around, and she opens it. Inside are two rows of beautiful, neatly placed red boutonnières. There are ten, one for each of the guys in our group.

"I got these for the guys," Mom says, smiling as she explains how to put them on the lapel of a suit jacket. "I think it would be nice if you put one on each of them."

There's a knock at the door. Mom opens it to reveal all the guys. They're looking like the most handsome pack of trouble I've ever seen, except for all the obvious injuries. They grin at us as Hiram and Arch catcall and whistle.

Mom carries the box out into the hall, where Presley, Val, Finley, and Kelsey start pinning flowers to each of their lapels. Unfortunately, I need help with Trey's because of my shoulder.

Rich steps out of the boys' room with a matching box full of corsages, and that's when Mom and Rich finally notice our collective damage.

As they look around at us, Rich's brow furrows. "What happened?" he asks. "You all look like you've been through a war."

We glance at each other. There's no hiding the evidence of the fight. Adam is heavily bandaged under his fitted dress shirt. Hiram has a bruise on his cheek. Val's lip is busted. Marcus is sporting a mean-looking bruise on his chin, and Arch's hand is wrapped because he broke two knuckles.

Mom zeroes in on me. "You've been favoring that shoulder all day."

I roll my eyes, frustrated, but Adam saves me from having to explain.

"Joel came to Hiram and Arch's party last night with reinforcements," he says. "Melanie's intuition gave us some warning, so we were ready for them. If it helps, they look worse than we do, and Joel's in jail on attempted-murder charges."

Mom gasps, her eyes wide. "Attempted murder?"

"Do any of you need to go to the hospital?" Rich asks.

We shake our heads.

"Everyone was checked by paramedics," Trey answers. "And I took Melanie to urgent care last night to get her shoulder checked.

It's inflamed, but nothing's broken or torn."

Mom regards Trey with a serious look. "You took her to the doctor?"

Trey winces. "Yes. You're going to get a hell of a bill. I'm sorry about that, but I had to know that she was okay."

Mom smiles, crosses the short distance, and hugs him. "We're not worried about the money. Thank you for taking care of her."

Surprised, Trey says, "I always will."

Mom and Rich exchange a look, and my intuition breathes through me. They've just figured out how serious things are between Trey and me.

Trey, Adam, Arch, Marcus, and Tanner step forward to take a wrist corsage out of the box Rich is holding. Mom and Rich came through again with the perfect touches to the evening.

Marcus's flip phone rings, and he answers it. We all watch, concerned, as his expression turns serious.

After a long moment, he says, "All right, Dad. I'll let them know."

He snaps the phone shut. "Joel's being held on attempted-murder charges." He looks my way. "I guess some old police reports were drudged up, and they're also going to revisit several previous attempted-rape charges. The detectives assigned to the case want to meet with all of us next week. If there's a trial, seems we're all going to have to testify."

We all exchange nervous glances.

Rich steps in. "I want all of you to listen to me. You've worked your tails off on this dance, and there's nothing anyone can do about the situation tonight. I want you to put it out of your minds and enjoy your evening. You've earned it. We can sort everything else out later."

"All right, everyone!" Arch says, trying to rally. "Our part's done, and the teacher chaperones have taken over all the rest of the work for the evening."

We all high-five, and the mood shifts festive.

"Rich and Carol, thank you for everything you did for us today." Adam shakes Rich's hand and hugs Mom. "We couldn't have done it without you. Thanks for arranging for us to have these rooms and for helping decorate the ballroom."

Everyone echoes the sentiment, and Arch points down the hall.

"We're out of here!" he says. "Let's go have the best night of our lives!"

Trey wraps an arm around my waist and steers me down the hall toward the elevators. "You're beautiful," he says, looking down at me with heat in his eyes. "I'm the luckiest guy in the world."

I lean into him. "You aren't so bad yourself. I love you."

Marcus and Presley move up beside us, and Marcus, batting his eyelashes like a cartoon character, leans in to Trey. "I love you too, you sexy devil, you."

Trey puts his arm around Marcus's shoulder and chuckles. "You know what, man? I'll take it!"

Everyone laughs.

"The history of this hotel is incredible," I say during the ride down in the elevator. "The first Academy Awards were held here, Marilyn Monroe lived here for two years, Shirley Temple rehearsed here, and Clark Gable and Charlie Chaplin stayed here."

Finley squeals. "Now we get to host a dance in the ballroom!"

We step off the elevator to the flash of camera bulbs. It's shocking for a split second until I remember we've hired actors to play the paparazzi. We all turn and grin at each other, then stroll up the red carpet, posing and smiling as we go.

Waiting at the end is the professional photographer. "All right, kids," he says. "Who's in the first picture?"

"All of us," Arch announces. "You can't split up this group. We ride together!"

So, how did it go? Well . . .

The dance was magic. Perfect music, perfect decorations, perfect food, and a perfect table of friends. We partied our asses off. We even got Adam out onto the dance floor, where, sporting his "penguin suit," he did the Roger Rabbit surrounded by a group of sweaty idiots.

Toward the end of the evening, Trey pulled me into the lobby and sat me down at the bar in the restaurant. I looked expectantly at the bartender, waiting for him to kick us out for being underage, but all he did was wink at me. Apparently, Trey arranged this in advance and got us permission to be there.

"Melanie," he said, "this is rumored to be where Marilyn Monroe was sitting when she met Arthur Miller. I want you to experience some of that magic. I brought you to this special place to give you this . . ." From his jacket pocket, he pulled out a black velvet jewelry-store box. He opened it, revealing a silver ring with black obsidian gems set in a delicate ornate pattern.

I looked up at him as he took the ring out of the box.

"We can't get married today or tomorrow," he said. "But until we can, this is a promise ring. So, Melanie, will you accept this ring as a promise of what's to come?"

My left hand trembled as I held it out. "The answer will always be yes."

He leaned in to kiss me as he slid the ring on my finger. Then he laced his hands with mine and sent a pulse that held fire and promise for the future.

The next day, Trey picked me up around lunch, and we drove to the beach. We made our way down the stairs to the sand and settled on our towels. I slipped off my flip-flops and wiggled my toes in the sand.

When my shoulder started throbbing, I removed the sling and stretched, working through some dance movement to try to relieve some of the stiffness.

Trey studied me. "You know, I've never seen you dance."

I laughed. "You danced with me to my favorite song, on Mulholland. We danced at my pool party. Then there was the homecoming dance just last night . . ."

He shook his head. "I mean I've never seen you *perform*. Demitri told me last week that you have remarkable ability. He's been really impressed with what he's seen you do in class."

I smiled appreciatively. "Coming from Demitri, that's a massive compliment. He's incredibly talented."

An idea flashed across Trey's face. "Dance." He smiled, gesturing to the open space in front of us.

"Here?"

He nodded.

"In the sand, on a crowded beach?"

"What's the harm? Go for it."

I laughed and shook my head. "You're insane."

"I'm serious. I want to see what all the fuss is about."

The old Melanie never would have considered dancing on a

public beach. She would have dismissed the idea immediately. But I found myself giving it genuine consideration.

"All right," I said. "I choreographed a solo after the laser show night. Skip to the next track on the CD."

He pressed a button on the boombox as I stood and took a few steps forward. Nervously, I turned to face him, my right foot popped and my head down. Oleta Adams's "Get Here" tinkled through the speaker. I slowly raised my head to gaze at him through the song's introduction. My right arm drifted up, my hand soft, as the lyrics started.

I worked through the choreography, some of it hazy in my memory. The good news about a solo is you can improvise and no one will know the difference.

I turned three times to the right, reaching to the side during the chime.

Slowly, I slid into the splits, holding the line a moment before rolling through a fan kick. I got to my knees and wafted my arms before I arched through my back, bringing my arms up and around. I glanced Trey's way and gave him a hint of a flirtatious smile before rolling over my shoulder and holding in an open split over my head before landing and pushing into a deep lunge.

A crowd gathered, but by that time there was no point in being shy.

I turned to face Trey, and he stood, mesmerized.

I smiled as the music built to a crescendo, and I jazz-ran his way, arms rising in front of me. I put my hands on his shoulders and extended my right leg, foot perfectly pointed. "Bend a little," I whispered to him.

He bent at the knees, and I hooked my extended leg over his shoulder.

"Hands on the small of my back," I told him.

He placed his hands, and I bent through my back, my head touching my standing leg.

"Straighten your knees."

When he straightened, I hung from his shoulder, my other foot off the ground.

"Pull me up slowly."

Smiling, he brought my back up.

"Now lift me onto your shoulder."

He raised me above him, so that I straddled his shoulder. My arms rose, my balance perfect. He set a hand on my leg to steady me, but I had this on my own.

I slid down the other side, my other leg rising, ending in a full split against his back. My right foot reached the sand, and I turned, fan-kicking my leg over with a sweep of my arm.

I turned along his back, taking his hands as I got to the front of him. "Tension in your arms."

He straightened them, and I leaned into a needle, my right leg at a perfect 180-degree angle. My leg slowly dropped, and I stood upright. I kissed him lightly before turning away and ending in a mermaid stance, reaching one hand delicately toward him. My head dropped softly at the end of the last note.

Our captive audience broke into applause.

A little girl ran to me, asking, "How do you do that?"

"I've been in dance classes every day for nine years," I told her.

"I'm Anna."

I grinned and introduced myself.

She turned to the man standing beside her. "Daddy, can I take dance classes?"

His eyebrows rose. "Absolutely."

When his daughter scampered off, the man turned to me. "I can't believe she just talked to you," he said, his tone surprised. "She's normally painfully shy. Her mom and I have been searching for ways to bring her out of her shell."

"Kids are intuitive," I said with a smile. "She knew I was a kindred spirit. I was just like her when I was little."

Trey came up behind me and set his hands on my shoulders.

"Thank you," Anna's dad said.

I nodded, and he walked back over to his family's spot on the beach.

"You just proved yet again that you're everything I want," Trey whispered. He turned me around. "That was seriously amazing."

I laughed and waved him off, still a little winded from the effort of dancing in the sand. It was a lot harder than dancing on a wood floor. "Thanks. Technically, I'm mediocre, at best, but I've got a strong connection to music. It compels me to perform." I gazed into his eyes. "It helps that the piece is about you."

He smiled and held out his hands, and I laced my fingers through his. He sent a pulse through our connection, and I closed my eyes to study it. It was a blend of all the things he loves about me. The emotions swirled with a faint image of me dancing.

I opened my eyes.

"I love you," he said.

I smiled softly, suddenly feeling a touch shy.

Trey looked thoughtful for a moment, then said, "When the laser show started, I was watching you from the corner of my eye. Your expression shifted through every emotion imaginable. I watched you instead of the show because I was so curious about you."

I blushed. "That's really sweet."

"Something happened in that moment, though," he continued. "These images started coming into my mind, but somehow, I knew they were more than imagination." He drew a long, slow breath. "In that moment, I saw our entire future together. I saw you becoming homecoming princess, our high school graduations. You're going to graduate in a white cap and gown, with honors. I saw us getting married. I saw our kids. We're going to have three, by the way. I saw us at Little League games, cheering on our youngest boy."

He quieted, and I let his words sink in. I'd be lying if I said they weren't shocking.

"Are you okay with all that?" I asked. "That's a lot for a teenage guy."

He smiled and shrugged. "Yes and no. I've never been a married-with-kids kind of daydreamer. So, in a way it was good because it helped me understand that this was something I needed to seriously pay attention to when it started. I admit that having that epiphany over a girl whose middle name I don't even know was scary."

I laughed. "It's Katherine."

"Well, good," Trey joked. "That solves that problem." He looked down at our entwined hands. "When you sent that first bolt of energy, it changed my life forever."

My breath caught, and my heart pounded. The world slipped away like it always does with Trey. He cupped my face and kissed me, sending fire up my spine. The energy hummed between us, braiding and melding. My head swam, and I realized that no matter how hard things get, I'll be okay because he's my other half.

When I pulled away, he tucked my hair behind my ear, then placed his fingertips on my forehead and ran them, featherlight, down my face to my chin. "I promise you that no matter what happens, I'm going to get you through it. But I'll let you do it your way."

As the sensation settled through me, I said, "Don't forget what you just did. It's perfect."

Special thanks to Carol Trueblood, Jordan Slocum, and Brian Dwyer for countless hours collaborating on conceptual details and proofreading; Candice Neu for use of Katharsis Media Studio; Angie Veal and Emily Armijo for reading the first draft and telling me to go for it.

MELISSA VELASCO is a choreographer, professor, dance teacher, author, stage manager, and Crystal Grid teacher. She enjoys the expansive views in her mountain home, especially when accompanied by a cup of hot tea and an entire day to write and choreograph. Her greatest loves are her three children and husband. The four pillars of her ultimate happiness include her family, friends, dance, and laughter.

THE HOLLYWOOD HIGH CHRONICLES

BOOK 2

Dark Water

Melanie's mind splinters as pressure mounts and she finds herself alone in a new metaphysical nightmare. Faced with the realities of her past and indecision about her future, a newfound side of herself takes over: her Dark Water side. Torn between right and wrong, good and evil, Trey and Adam, the time has come for Melanie to sink or swim.

9 781736 537350